P9-DYE-281

# BANG

## A NOVEL

## BARRY LYGA

LITTLE, BROWN AND COMPANY
New York   Boston

Copyright © 2017 by Barry Lyga
Discussion Guide copyright © 2017 by Little, Brown and Company

Cover design by Marcie Lawrence.
Cover art copyright © 2018 by Neil Swaab. Lettering by gray318.
Cover copyright © 2018 by Hachette Book Group, Inc.

Little, Brown and Company
Hachette Book Group
1290 Avenue of the Americas, New York, NY 10104
Visit us at LBYR.com

Originally published in hardcover and ebook by Little, Brown and Company in April 2017
First Trade Paperback Edition: September 2018

Little, Brown and Company is a division of Hachette Book Group, Inc.
The Little, Brown name and logo are trademarks of Hachette Book Group, Inc.

The publisher is not responsible for websites (or their content) that are not owned by the publisher.

The Library of Congress has cataloged the hardcover edition as follows:
Names: Lyga, Barry, author.
Title: Bang : a novel / by Barry Lyga.
Description: First Edition. | New York ; Boston : Little, Brown and Company, 2017. | Summary: A new friend and their YouTube cooking channel help fourteen-year-old Sebastian move on from accidentally shooting his infant sister ten years earlier.
Identifiers: LCCN 2016019843| ISBN 9780316315500 (hardcover) | ISBN 9780316315531 (ebook) | ISBN 9780316315524 (library edition ebook)
Subjects: | CYAC: Guilt—Fiction. | Friendship—Fiction. | Family problems—Fiction. | Single-parent families—Fiction. | YouTube (Electronic resource)—Fiction.
Classification: LCC PZ7.L97967 Ban 2017 | DDC [Fic]—dc23
LC record available at https://lccn.loc.gov/2016019843

ISBNs: 978-0-316-31551-7 (pbk.), 978-0-316-31553-1 (ebook)

Printed in the United States of America

LSC-C

10  9  8  7  6  5  4  3  2  1

# PRAISE FOR
## *Bang*

### A YALSA Best Fiction for Young Adults Pick

"**Affecting**, and unfortunately **timely**, *Bang* is a read that's worth your inevitable heartbreak." —*Entertainment Weekly*

"Lyga captures the heartbreak of Sebastian's situation with **sensitivity and compassion**, exploring how a life can be unfairly defined by just one action, how it's tragically easy to ignore humanity in favor of a headline, and just what communication, love and sharing the truth can do, especially when it comes to forgiving oneself." —*The New York Times*

★ "**Heartbreaking** and brutally **compelling**."
—*Kirkus Reviews*, starred review

★ "**A raw exploration** of persistent social stigmas, **a beautiful study** of forgiveness, and an unflinching portrait of a parent's worst nightmare." —*Publishers Weekly*, starred review

★ "Lyga tackles a number of relevant issues in this heartbreaking novel, including gun control, suicide, and religious and racial prejudice. The pain and anguish Sebastian feels every day are raw and chafing, and the chemistry between Sebastian and Aneesa is **tender and realistic**." —*SLJ*, starred review

★ "Painfully raw and accented with hope and anguish, *Bang* will connect solidly with older teens looking for **a deep and affecting story**." —*Shelf Awareness*, starred review

"Lyga manages his **intensely emotional** material well, creating in Sebastian a highly empathetic character." —*Booklist*

"*Bang* **draws readers in from the first page** and holds them captive." —*VOYA*

"The emotions are **effectively detailed**." —*The Bulletin*

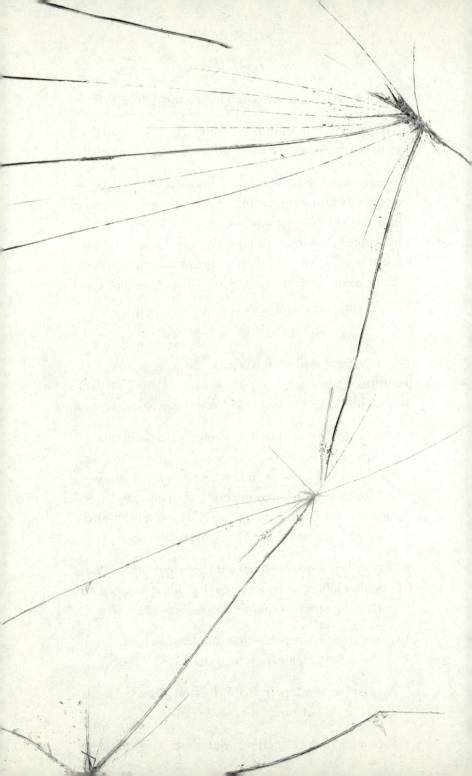

*For M & B,*
*loves of my life*

And the thing is this:
I don't even remember doing it.

# History

**My sister is in the memory hole.**

She has been disappeared, vanished, eliminated, eradicated. The memory hole is a conceit from a book they made us read in school, *1984*. Even though the story takes place in the past, it feels very much like the present or the near future. It feels like something incipient, imminent, pervasive. Like a fog so cold it's a thousand needles in your skin, just barely breaking the surface.

*1984* is a full-body tattoo that's about to start, and it bestowed upon me the memory hole, which swallowed my sister bodily ten years ago.

There are no photos of her in the house.

There is no scrapbook. No baby clothes or stuffed animals or bright, crocheted baby blankets.

She's been extinguished. She's been erased.

My sister is in the memory hole because I killed her.

**I'm told it was a Tuesday. I'm told it was June and it** was hot and there'd been no rain for weeks, no respite from the heat that pressed down on Brookdale. I'm told Mom was in the backyard, hanging laundry on the line, that my father was in the garage.

I'm told I leveled my father's .357 Magnum at her as she sat in the little bouncy chair with the stuffed birds hanging overhead. I'm told she would only nap in the bouncy chair, that she loved the stuffed birds and the birdsong that the chair played for her.

I'm told it was point-blank range and that I shot her one time.

Which, really, is all it takes.

She was four months old.

I'm told.

I'm told Mom got there first, the back door being close to the nursery. My father arrived a few seconds later and I was on the floor, blacked out from the kick of the pistol, which knocked me across the room. I'm told Mom screamed and screamed, clawing at her face at the sight before her. Local legend has it that my father, fearing she would gouge her own eyes out or tear her face to ribbons, deliberately punched her out cold.

I have no reason not to believe any of the things I've been told.

I'm told so many things.

I was a child. It was an accident. It wasn't my fault.

I'm told.

I was four years old.

**It was ten years ago and it's June now, again, as it** is every year, but it's not a Tuesday, but it is ten years to the day, and it's going to rain, my phone tells me. It's going to rain.

Good.

Good.

I like the rain. I like it ferocious and I like it gentle. I like sudden showers that last the afternoon and sprinkles that don't last the time it takes to run to the car.

Rain is *clean*.

It's Sunday and the last week of school starts tomorrow, so I stare out the window and ignore my homework, and I think of lightning, and of thunder, and of the rain.

There's no indication it's been ten years, no sign of the morbid anniversary. Mom is no more or less morose on this day—she wears her sadness always, an unseeable, unavoidable mantle.

She goes to bed early this night, but Mom frequently goes to bed early, a glass of wine in her hand or—sometimes—a too-sweet scent drifting up from under her closed bedroom door.

Every night before bed, she seeks me out wherever in the house I happen to be and kisses the top of my head. These days, this requires that I be sitting or that she take my face in her hands and tilt my head down. Tonight is a tilting night, as I'm standing at the window.

She pecks at my hairline and says, "I love you."

I don't know when this ritual began. Some nights, she says it perfunctorily; others, sweetly; still others, dully. Tonight, she says it with difficulty, as though she's a child who's broken a neighbor's window and has been forced by a parent to apologize.

"I'm sorry," I want to say, but don't. Every time my mother tells me she loves me, this is what I want to say.

**That night, after dark, before the rain, I sneak out** of the house. I've mastered this particular skill over the course of many dead nights, when the silence is too loud and the solitude too confining. Mom sleeps soundly and well and without break. I sneak out of the house, but the truth is, I could simply *leave*.

I ride my bike out of the neighborhood, out to where Route 27 intersects Brook Road. The night is overcast, but the streetlights and a gauzy blur of moonlight show the way. The remnants of the day's heat and humidity linger like party guests who stubbornly refuse to get the hint.

The streets are empty, except for the occasional rumble of a big rig dinosauring from out of the darkness back into the darkness. I sail through intersections, the traffic lights gone blinking red after midnight.

Halfway there, the rain timidly speaks up, beginning as a hanging mist. Moisture wicks by; jewels grow on my eyelashes, distorting the meager light. I wipe at them; they grow back like Hydra heads.

Soon, the mist breaks, maturing into a light tattoo of soft, nearly soundless droplets. Sweat mingles, and a thread of moisture runs cold against the warm skin of the back of my neck, beneath my shirt collar and down my back. Lifting my feet from the pedals, I coast onto the shoulder, then bump and jostle onto the grass, gliding down a grade. My tires, rain-grass slick, slip and jitter under me. I wrestle them under control almost unconsciously.

Through a stand of trees, I see it. Drifting to a halt as the grade levels, I lean my bike against an aging poplar, its branches bent, gnarled, as though arthritic and melancholy. I pick my way through an undergrowth of sticker bushes and brambles.

Above, the rain patters on the leaves.

Ahead, it crouches in the dark, a deader dark, cloaked in dirt and rust.

The old mobile home seems to tilt just slightly to the left, but this is an illusion caused by a dent in the roof and the natural slope of the land here. It is still and silent, save for the clink and ping of raindrops, audible even from here.

This is where.

This is where it will happen.

This is where I will do it.

When the time comes.

I've fired a gun once in my life.

I'll do it again.

When the time comes.

# The Present

**My best friend is Evan Danforth.** "Of the Brookdale Danforths," he likes to joke, speaking through and down his nose. His parents are absurdly rich, "offensively rich," Evan often says, snorting as though money is something to be ashamed of, something to hide and conceal. His parents hate that he takes the bus to school, and they hate that he's friends with me.

Sometimes I wonder if Evan does those things in spite of his parents or because of them.

We're a sort of yin and yang of rich and not-rich. Randomly assigned to a homework project together in the bygone days of elementary school, bonding over a mutual love of Power Rangers and Hostess apple pies. On such flimsy foundations are best friendships built.

My therapist, Dr. Kennedy, once told me, "That's what makes them best friendships."

As usual, Evan is saving a seat for me on the bus, and I slide in. Another year down. Ten years. No one said anything. No one ever says anything. Nothing online. Nothing in the

Sunday edition of the *Lowe County Times*—"the Loco"—that Mom still has delivered every week.

Memory holes are efficient.

"One more week," Evan groans. "If we didn't have all that snow, we'd be out by now."

"It's just a week."

"A week out of our young lives," he says. "We'll never get this week back."

"Your parents can buy you another week."

He splutters laughter. Evan's laughter, even when surprised and uncontrolled, is musical and clear, unlike my own, which is rare and snorty and mucus-y.

Rich people can afford anything, even better laughter.

"Even Richard and Myra can't buy time," he tells me. "I bet they'd try, though."

Richard Danforth is a hunter. A "gentleman hunter," Evan's mom says. He owns expensive rifles and shotguns, stocks inlaid with silver and mother-of-pearl. Titanium triggers and blued steel barrels that he polishes twice a season. He's NRA. He votes Republican. "For financial reasons."

Myra Danforth is patrician and WASP-y, with an immaculate coif of frosty blond hair that comes just to her chin and breasts that she holds high and enhanced. "Fortieth birthday present," Evan muttered to me once. I've never seen her smile—the closest I've ever witnessed is a slight upturn of one corner of her mouth. I don't know if

14

she's extra-reserved in my presence or if she's just incapable of smiling. Botox or genetics or disposition—who knows?

She's not a MILF. Because I wouldn't want to go anywhere near her, even though I admit I've fantasized about her more than once. There's a difference between what you'll do in your mind and what you'll actually do for real.

I think of those perfectly sculpted breasts and I realize Evan's wrong—rich people *can* buy time. Or a decent replica. They can stall it, put it off, freeze it, while the rest of us just lurch along with our snorty laughs into our inevitable futures.

"You should come over today," Evan is saying while I'm silently judging his family. "Downloaded the demo for *Stark Weather* this morning."

"I have some stuff I have to do," I tell him.

"Like what?"

I invent an excuse—something about a dentist appointment—and he drops it. A few seconds later, I happen to catch his reflection in the bus window as he drops his eyelids and grimaces. He's my best friend, so I've seen this before, and I know what it is—silent recrimination. He's making the connection. Shooting games. Me. Guns. He's figured it out, and he's angry at himself for not thinking it through beforehand.

Not his fault, though. It's not as though I wear a sign saying, *I killed my sister with a gun, so don't ask me to play your super-realistic first-person shooter*. No one else needs to feel bad about what happened. Only one person.

I wish there were a way to assuage him, a way to tell him, *It's all right. You don't have to step around the rusty nails and broken glass of my past. Don't beat yourself up.* But the only way to do that would be to acknowledge it in the first place, to say it happened, and I can't do that. When I try to talk about it, everything goes haywire. In Dr. Kennedy's office, I was okay, for some reason. He made it okay. But otherwise...

But Evan is my best friend, so I do what I can, which is give him a way out.

"Besides, you know me—I'm no good at the new games."

"That's true," he says with a small grin.

But for the rest of the ride to school, Evan sits in silence, kicking himself. I, too, sit in silence, letting him.

I'm no good at the new games because I rarely play them.

I like old things.

Old books.

Old movies.

Old TV shows.

It's not that life seemed simpler "back then." It's that it was more complicated. When no one had a cellphone, it was harder to get in touch with people. You called a phone number, and you might get the person you wanted to talk to...or her dad. Or mom. Or brother. And without the Internet, simple questions could mean a trip to the library, hours in the stacks.

Life was more complicated, but it was quieter, I bet. Slower. And the distractions were not the ephemeral flash of an Instagram as it scrolled by or the blurt of a tweet. No endless chattering of Facebook status updates and Snapchats and notifications pushed to your tablet, your computer, your phone, your watch.

The distractions then were card catalogs and dust and the smell of old paper and ink. The distractions were deep.

I wonder what it would be like to go back in time, to live as long ago as the 1980s, or even further back.

To know what was to come.

On the way home that day, I stare out the bus window. Evan has been dropped off already, and I am alone in my seat as the bus wends its way slowly toward my bus stop. I catch sight of a large truck—a moving van, I realize—parked in the driveway of a house that has been on the market for so many months that I assumed it would never sell. Two dark-skinned men—one in a dress shirt and a tie fluttering in the breeze, one in blue coveralls— argue, gesturing angrily at each other, at the house, at the van. On the porch, a slender figure in black watches, and I think I notice something, but then we're farther down the road and whatever I thought I noticed is gone.

Mom is still at work when I get home, so I go to what had been my sister's room, the nursery. I only go in when Mom isn't home.

In movies and on TV, when someone's child dies, they almost always show the room preserved, frozen in time. In English class, I learned that this sort of thing is supposed to be *symbolic*, that the room's unchanging appearance reflects the inability of the parents to move on, the rigid, frozen horror and pain that cannot thaw.

This is why I've come to the conclusion that symbolism is bullshit. Because my sister's room is *not* preserved, but no one has moved on. We're all still stuck in place.

The room serves now as storage. There are boxes and bags of things here, most of them belonging to my father, things my mother won't throw out. Not out of sentiment— out of spite. "I won't do his dirty work for him," she said once. "His things will rot in there before I lift a finger to get rid of them."

It made no sense to me then and makes no sense to me now, but I try to avoid asking my mother to explain herself.

For a time, I thought the boxes and the bags might contain mementos of my sister—photos, old toys, old clothes. But, no. There are books and magazines, old drawings, bits and pieces of model airplanes and HO scale trains. I have a vague, flickering memory of a Christmas tree scraping the ceiling and a model train platform that took up half the living room floor, the chug and click of the train cars in unison with sparks that delighted me. One engine almost politely burped puffs of smoke. The smell of pine, the stab-crunch of needles underfoot through winter-thick socks. A giggle-laugh that must have been mine.

A broken chunk of old memory, adrift in a pool of blood.

I don't want to remember it. Memories go into the memory hole. That's where they belong. Dr. Kennedy thought that if I could remember the shooting, I could move on from it. I told him I didn't want that in my head, just like I don't want my father's trains and the smell of pine.

Our Christmas tree for the past few years has been a four-foot-tall plastic and aluminum facsimile of a fir that Mom has me haul out of the attic shortly after each Thanksgiving. It looks as fresh each year as the year before. My sister's room is not frozen in time, but the Christmas tree is. It's still not symbolic, though—it's just crappy Chinese plastic. It's chemistry class, not English.

There may be symbols and symbolism in books and movies—sometimes it's even fun to find them—but in real life, we only have boxes and bags, old sagging shelves, and attics with fake Christmas trees. And none of it means anything. It's all just the detritus of life, our own jetsam, heaved overboard, then washed back to us by the waves and the tides.

Coming around and around again. And the water disgorges the same sights, same house, same me, same Mom.

# My Mom

My mom is forty-one years old. She does not nec-essarily look older than that, but the fact is that *forty-one* is usually people's second or third guess after two higher numbers. Not substantially higher—they guess forty-three, maybe, then wince at the flicker in her eyes that says *too high* and drop to forty-one.

When people get older, they develop fine crenellations around their eyes, typically called crow's feet or, more pop-ularly, smile lines.

In my mother's case, I don't believe they were caused by smiling.

She conceals her sadness as well as could be expected, ten years later. She laughs at silly sitcoms and she grins at funny comments her friends leave on Facebook, but there is always a veil between her mirth and the world, a sheer scrim that mutes her reaction. It is as though she is a half second behind the world and can never catch up. And has given up trying.

I try to stay out of her way. This is just something I do. I avoid her. I began doing this early on. Some of my earliest memories. Six or seven years old and I was trying not to spend time around my own mother.

I don't want her to see me too often, to encounter me, to deal with me. Me, this walking, talking, living, breathing, eating, shitting, farting reminder of what she's had and what she's lost. During the school year, it's easy—I'm out the door after she leaves for work and most days I've eaten dinner and ensconced myself in my bedroom by the time she's home.

Summer, it's harder. With no ready-made excuse for being absent, I look for ways to get out. I don't linger in the house. I sleep in late, stay out late, keep my bedroom door closed when I'm home.

I make myself invisible, intangible.

It's easier for her, easier for me, just easier, period.

According to Dr. Kennedy, my mother is the surviving member of the family dealing with my sister's death the best. Let that tell you something.

**There are ingredients in the refrigerator for pizza.** This is Mom's unspoken, unspeaking way of telling me that I should make pizza for dinner. I typically make something for myself before she comes home, but some days she requests homemade pizza. It's what we have that passes for tradition.

I assembled my first homemade pizza three years ago, when I was eleven. In a mandatory home ec class in middle school, we made French bread pizzas, twenty-one eleven- and twelve-year-olds slopping sauce onto bread, sprinkling plasticky shredded mozzarella over it, then shoving the whole dripping mess into the school's ovens.

Somehow, this fascinated me. The too-browned, soggy results of the culinary experiment resembled actual pizza closely enough that I was captivated, stunned that something hitherto conjured only from a cardboard delivery box could be brought into existence with my own two hands. It was all I talked about for days, until Mom finally bowed to my insistence and allowed me to make pizza for lunch one Saturday.

The results were less impressive than in home ec, as impossible as that seemed, and Mom declared that we would henceforth "do this right." She downloaded a guide to making homemade pizza, and my obsession was born. I wanted to go back to the beginning, to the raw ingredients. I learned how to use the big stand mixer and make my own dough. I sliced the slightly gelatinous bulbs of mozzarella. While at first I used store-bought sauce, I eventually unearthed a good and not-too-difficult recipe online and began making my own. I wanted to smoke my own meats for sausage and pepperoni, but Mom drew the line there.

From the ingredients she's assembled, tonight looks like pesto and chicken pizza, one of my favorites. The dough ball is already thawed in the fridge; I like the sensation of kneading it, its elasticity, its pliability. I flour the counter and roll out a crust measuring about fourteen inches across. Just enough for two people. I crimp the edges with my fingers.

I slice mozzarella into discs. Shredding it gives a more even coverage, but I like the look of the slices after they've melted. I chop the chicken and scrounge in the fridge for the remains of an onion. Mom always forgets the onion. "You can just use onion powder," she likes to say, but it's not the same. Not at all.

I sauté the chicken and onion together in some olive oil, toss in some fresh grated pepper, and preheat the oven as high as it can go.

The pesto—*not* homemade, I regret; Mom still hasn't bought a food processor—gets spooned onto the crust first. A little goes a long way. I want just a glistening sheen of green and black, not a sludge. Then I add the slices of mozzarella, aiming for maximum coverage without any sort of noticeable pattern.

The chicken and onions go on last. *Almost* last. After they're distributed across the pie, something looks off, so I grate some parmesan and sprinkle it over the whole thing.

That works.

I crank out my homework while the oven finishes preheating. There's little to do this late in the year, so it doesn't take long.

My culinary pride and joy—a pizza stone Mom bought me for Christmas last year—rests hot and ready on the center rack of the oven. First I sprinkle it with a little cornmeal (to keep the crust from sticking) and then, with a pizza peel, I transfer my creation to the stone.

The pizza's done by the time Mom walks in the door ten minutes later, the cheese bubbling and perfectly pocked with brown, the crust tanned and only the slightest bit yielding.

"Your timing is impeccable," Mom says, pecking me on the forehead. I wait until she turns around to put her purse down before rubbing the kiss-spot on my forehead with the palm of my hand.

"It needs a couple of minutes to cool," I remind her as I paddle the pizza out of the oven and set it on the counter. "Otherwise the cheese will go all over the place when I cut it."

"Well, I'll go wash up and get out of these shoes."

A few minutes later, we're at the table, eating in silence. I would rather be watching TV. Or eating alone.

But I just eat. Because there are things we do.

"This is really good," Mom says, and I grunt, "Uh-huh," because if I say nothing, she gets angry, and I don't like to make her angry. Not because of anything she does or says when she's angry, but just because making her angry makes me sad. She doesn't deserve it.

"It really hits the spot," she goes on.

"Uh-huh."

There's a familiar tone in her voice. It's the *I have something to say, but I don't want to just jump right into it, so I'll do chit-chat first* tone. I know it well.

"Sebastian, could you at least *look* at me when I talk to you?"

With a slow, infinite effort, I lift my gaze to her. She smiles that gauzy smile.

"Was that so difficult?"

"Compared to what?"

The smile widens almost imperceptibly. "I think we should talk."

"Isn't that what we're doing right now? Have I been misled my whole life?"

"I'm thinking we should talk about what you're going to do this summer."

A shrug. "I'll get by."

"No. I don't want you lazing around like last summer."

"Last summer was pretty great. I didn't laze. I was hanging out with Evan."

"And what did you two accomplish?"

Touché.

"You're fourteen now. Old enough to get a summer job." Before I can protest too vociferously, she forestalls me with a raised palm. "Or do *something* productive. It doesn't have to be a job. Just something worthwhile."

"Evan isn't getting a job." Evan will be headed to something called Young Leaders Camp, a hellish mix of Model UN and overnight camp, spliced with the DNA of a tech start-up incubator. It's what rich kids do with their idle time as they await their Ivy League acceptance letters and keys to the Congressional washroom.

This is an argument I know is doomed to immediate failure, and—truth be told—I only offer it halfheartedly.

Mom doesn't disappoint. The words *rich*, *family*, and *not the same* are employed rather effectively in a mix of others.

"I want you to know how proud I am of you," Mom says slowly, so slowly that I almost believe her. "You take care of yourself. You aren't mixed up in anything crazy. I don't have to worry about you."

*Anymore*, I add silently.

"But you're in high school and you're going to be a sophomore. You're going to graduate sooner than you think. And I'm not saying that you need to figure your life out right here, right now, or even this summer, but, Sebastian... honey, you need to start at least *thinking* about it."

I shrug. A shrug is, by definition, a noncommittal action, but I do my best to add further noncommitment to it. I don't want to think about or *start* thinking about figuring out my life, for whatever it's worth.

"You can't drift your whole life. You can't give up on your future because of what happened—"

And almost without realizing, I'm telling her to shut up.

And she won't, so I'm telling her to seriously *shut up*, to shut her big fat stinking mouth, and she's a blur through my tears and I can't hear her voice through my own yelling—

—I don't know when I started yelling—

—as I'm up from the table—

—running—

—bathroom—

—just in time—

—tears and snot and then leaning over the toilet, vomiting chicken and pesto and mozz and parm and the crust, all of it gone, a green-gray sludge floating there as I spit the last bits into the water, crouched down, clinging to the tank and the rim of the bowl as though I could fall in and drown.

28

**I flush.**

I rinse my mouth with lukewarm water cupped in my hands. I spit out grit that tastes of garlic and basil.

Wipe my eyes. My mouth. Blow my nose.

Mom loiters in the hallway, waiting for me as I emerge. A glut of emotions roils inside me. I'm ashamed of yelling at her, of running away, of throwing up. I'm furious at her for bringing up the past. I'm outraged. I'm exhausted.

On those rare occasions that I dredge up our shared history, she suddenly comes down with a migraine. Or a stomachache. Anything to avoid the topic.

"You can't do this to me," I tell her. "When *I* try to talk about it, you decide it's not time. But then you go and spring it on me. It's not fair."

"This isn't over," she says quietly. "By the weekend, I want you to be able to sit down and tell me your plans for the summer."

I tell her to fuck off.

I tell her I can't think straight.

I tell her to go to hell.

I tell her I'll do it.

I tell her I can't do it.

I tell her it's pointless.

I tell her none of those things. Because I can't believe she's still fixated on me having a "productive" summer. If I'd had an aneurysm instead, if I'd had a heart attack, if I'd collapsed twitching into an epileptic fit, *then* would she understand how desperately I do not intend to have this conversation? Or would she run alongside my stretcher as it's borne into an ambulance, lecturing me on the importance of my future?

But that's all pointless speculation. Because this summer will be my last. And that, most likely, is why I really reacted the way I did. Because it's true and it's coming and it's happening, and she's acting like this is just any other summer.

Not that she knows. Not that I can tell her.

"I'm going to ride my bike," I tell her.

"Be back before ten," she says. "It's a school night," she adds needlessly, as though I can't tell on my own.

I say nothing. Outside, the sun is setting, the air still humid. Muggier than usual, the day's heat releasing last night's rain from the soil into the air.

I take off from the back of the house, cutting through the Marchettis' backyard too fast for Mr. Marchetti to notice it's me and yell from his window.

On an adrenaline high, I lose control of my bike in the dark. A patch of slick grass over mud. The next thing I know, I've wiped out for the first time since I was six, my bike slipping out from under me and dumping me onto the wet ground.

"Are you okay?" A girl's voice.

I *was* okay, until I realized my private humiliation was actually a public exhibition. The voice comes from the back porch of a house. Not just any house, though—it's the house where I watched the mover arguing with the new owner.

A dark shape moves, backlit by the porch light. I hold up a hand to eclipse the glare. "I'm fine."

"Are you sure?" she asks.

"Yeah." I lever myself off the ground, then I realize I've planted one hand on the muddy spot for support. With a sigh, I flap the hand, shaking off the mud. I'll have to wipe it on my pants.

"Don't do that," she says suddenly, reading my mind. Or, more likely, my body language. There's a clatter of feet on steps, and then she's right there, right in front of me, holding out a handkerchief, and I try not to stare at the scarf wound around her head. It's not that I've never seen this before. I've just never seen it live, in person. Especially here, in Brookdale, the place crowned three years ago as the "Whitest Town in Maryland."

"Want a picture?" she asks. Not testily, to her credit and to my shame.

"I'm sorry." I take the handkerchief and focus mightily on the complex task of wiping my hands clean. When I look up to return her handkerchief, I can't help but stare at her, all light brown skin and quirked lips and arched eyebrows.

"I'm Sebastian." I hold out a now-clean hand in what suddenly feels like a retrograde and archaic gesture.

The hand hangs there in the air for a too-long moment. She considers it, hesitates. I withdraw my hand, which now burns as though it's been caught at something.

"I'm sorry," I blurt out immediately. "Really sorry."

She laughs and the tension evaporates, just like that. "You're apologizing for what *I* did? Do you always do that?"

"I don't know." And I don't. But I don't care. I don't care about anything. I can't believe that I'm standing here, talking to her. Her face is almost perfectly round, utterly smooth, bordered by the scarf such that there's nothing to distract from those eyes, from *her*. No ears, no hair, no earrings or neck. Just that face and that gaze. She could have asked me if I always climb the waterspout to the rooftop during a full moon, and I would have said, "I don't know."

It's not that I'm smitten. Or in love. I am, rather, stunned. Last year in Advanced English Lit, we read part of an old, old poem called *Paradise Lost*. In it, the word *astonied* was used, which apparently is similar to *astounded*, but it has to do with turning to stone from shock. Metaphorically. And right now, I am *astonied*.

Wait. How long has it been since I said anything? What's wrong with me?

"I'm Sebastian." I tell her, not offering my hand.

"You said. I'm Aneesa."

"Aneesa."

"Yep."

I say it one more time, tasting it before letting it spill out of my mouth. "What does it mean?" I ask, and immediately feel like a jackass, because isn't that what people always say to people with foreign-sounding names? Ugh.

She stares, irritation and insouciance dancing together in those blacker-than-black eyes. "I'll tell you," she says, not unkindly, "if you can tell me what *your* name means."

"It's . . . it's just a name." I hand back the handkerchief. We don't actually touch, but for a moment we're both touching the cloth. This conversation is officially off to a screeching halt. I let go of the handkerchief, and my hand suddenly feels lonely.

"Thanks for the handkerchief," I say as lamely as humanly possible. "Good luck moving in."

"'Good luck moving in'? Is the house haunted? Is the neighborhood watch coming after us?"

"I saw your dad arguing with the mover, is all."

"Oh. Right." She shrugs. "They left something like three boxes at the old house. And they were like, 'It's our policy that another truck will redeliver in two days.' And Dad said, 'It's not Timbuktu—it's Baltimore. It's literally less than an hour away. Just go get them.'"

"So what happened?" I don't know why I care. This is the most boring anecdote I could ever imagine. Yet I'm captivated for some reason. Astonied.

"Dad got on the phone with the people at the office and sounded all confused and said something like, 'Am I really supposed to tip these guys for not getting the job done?' And the guy with the truck was suddenly like, 'We'll go get those boxes.' And they did." At the end of her tale, she smiles dimples into her cheeks and spreads her hands as though she's just performed a magic trick. Even though it's just a Story About Some Boxes, I can't help it—I grin back at her, as though we've just conquered high-level algebra together.

"I'm glad that turned out well for you."

She shrugs again. "It was three boxes of kitchen stuff. No big."

In the ensuing silence, I realize I'm staring at her and that she is, of course, intensely aware of this. I could stare even longer, but it could become more uncomfortable than it already is, if that's even possible. I stoop for my bike, right it, and throw a leg over. "Well, I guess I'll see you at school. Or on the bus. You're in high school, right?"

"Yeah. But I finished freshman year at my old school, so I won't start up again until fall."

"Lucky you."

And I ride off.

I actually ride off on that.

*Lucky you.*

I am genuinely stupid.

**By the time I've coasted down the hill off of Route 27** and stashed my bike among the trees, I've forgotten all about Aneesa and her kitchen boxes, her sly dad, her dimples, and my *Lucky you*.

I lurk at the tree line, staring out at the rusty hulk of the trailer. Then, gnawing on my lower lip, I sink to the ground and sit and contemplate my plan.

When I'm with other people, I usually don't think about it. Sometimes, it catches me off-guard, but I usually don't.

When I'm alone, it's *all* I can think about.

**Later, I slip into the house. Mom watches TV on the** sofa. It's ten after ten, but she says nothing, rising and turning off the TV before heading to her room without a word.

It's something of a tradition in my house, albeit involuntary, that on the last day of school, I come home and collapse on my bed and fall into a deep sleep. I don't know why this happens. As long as I can remember, though, that last day of school exhausts me beyond my limits, and I have no choice but to crash. In previous years, I've attempted caffeine boosts late in the day, loud music, and other stimulants, only to succumb to my bed each time.

By the time I'd waken, groggy and out of sorts, Mom would be home with take-out Chinese and a bottle of the organic root beer I like that you can only get at the grocery store near her job. We'd toast to another year down, and I'd gorge myself on moo goo gai pan, egg rolls, brown rice, and crab rangoon.

But this year and this last day, I happen to spy Aneesa sitting on her front porch as the bus trundles past her house. When I get home, my bed seems miles away, even as I toss my near-empty backpack onto it. Without so much as a yawn or a stretch, I wheel my bike out of the garage and take off up Fox Tail Drive.

She's still sitting outside, loitering, shielded from the sun by the porch overhang. The house looks mostly the same; the Realtor's sign still lurks at the end of the drive-way, a bright red SOLD add-on attached to the top. Like most of the houses in this neighborhood, it's two stories, shingled (in light blue with buttery yellow shutters), with a narrow porch and a one-car garage. Also like most of the houses in this neighborhood—including mine—the cars are parked in the driveway.

*Lucky you* was the last thing I said to her. I don't know how it hit her ears: snarky, sincere, flippant, whatever. But she's new and she's cute and she talked to me and I said *Lucky you* and pedaled off into the night.

I get to the end of Aneesa's driveway and lift my hand to wave to her when it occurs to me that I have absolutely no idea what I'm doing. Am I going to cruise past and casu-ally wave as I go? If so, where am I headed, and how long do I have to stay there until it doesn't look odd for me to come back? Or am I stopping here, in which case . . . why? What am I going to say? Why am I doing this? What the hell am I thinking?

I've been riding a bike since age five, to the point where it's one of those tasks that once seemed complicated but has evolved into reflexive second nature. That doesn't stop me from becoming so distracted with my own brain that I nudge the handlebars in one direction as I lean in another, causing the whole thing to wobble (no doubt comically to an observer) before dumping me without ceremony—or dignity—right at the lip of Aneesa's driveway.

Just to drive home the shame of it, I hear myself yelp, "Hey!" at least three octaves higher than my usual voice. Not a growly, manly "Shit!" or a grunt or even just stoic, resigned silence. No, not me. I have to explode in a shrieky, shrill "Hey!"

The next thing I know, Aneesa is right there, hovering over me.

"I'm fine," I tell her before she can say anything, before I can even be certain it's true. "I'm okay." She's extended her hand, but I brush it off.

"Are you sure? You look a little shaky. Should I call an ambulance?"

An ambulance? God, no. "I'm fine."

"Or my dad can drive you—"

"I'm okay. Honest." I take inventory—scraped knee, banged-up elbow. No damage to my head. No tears in my clothes. Pride, self-respect, dignity: seriously sprained.

To my chagrin, I realize that I'm sort of tangled up in the bike, and I need that hand of hers after all.

Last night, she wouldn't shake. Today she's helping me up. Progress?

"Maybe you shouldn't ride a bike anymore," she says. "You're not very good at it."

I check that I'm okay to stand, not too wobbly. There are smears of blood on both legs, but that's it. "I'm fine at it."

"I've seen you on it twice and you've wiped out twice."

"You're not around the millions of times I manage not to fall off."

"I'm not sure I can trust you on this."

"Who would lie about riding a bike?"

"Someone who can't." She takes a few steps toward the house and nods in its general direction. "C'mon. Let's put some stuff on your cuts."

"I don't need—"

"—an infection," she says triumphantly. "Exactly what I was thinking."

I sigh heavily and drag my bike—which seems to have survived with less damage than I have—onto her yard, then follow her into the house.

"A guy died here," she says as we cross the threshold. Her tone is casual, but I can tell she's very serious about it. "He was really old, and he had a stroke in the shower."

"I know. I didn't think anyone would ever buy this house."

"Can you believe people worry about that?"

I decide to treat it as a rhetorical question. Inside, the man I saw arguing with the mover—Aneesa's dad—hunches over an entertainment center, untangling a snakes' nest of cables. He's wearing khakis and a light blue dress shirt, the sleeves rolled up to reveal slender but powerful forearms.

"Dad, Sebastian. Sebastian, Dad." Aneesa doesn't even wait for her dad to turn around before she goes pounding up a flight of stairs.

Rolling his sleeves down to his wrists, her dad turns to me, flicks his gaze to my bloody shins. "Don't bleed on the carpet. My wife'll kill me."

He has a light tone to his voice and no accent. Why did I expect an accent? I don't know. But there's none.

I dutifully step off the carpet and onto a collapsed cardboard box in case there's any drippage.

"Perfect," he says, and returns his attention to the endless tangle of cables.

"There's a trick to it," I offer.

He narrows his eyes. "You're not suggesting the Alexandrian solution, I hope."

"No, sir. I left my sword at home."

With a chuckle, he rises and hands the ball of cables to me. "Anyone who knows his mythology that well, I trust with my cables."

I take the ball as he settles into a comfortable-looking armchair. The first trick to untangling a wad of cables like this is figuring out which one will come out easiest. So you identify the two ends of each cable and eyeball which one has the fewest bends and knots in it. Start there, and you immediately clear some of the path to cable free-dom. I begin with a red HDMI cable, working it carefully through a maze of twists and kinks.

"Sebastian, was it?" he says, watching me. "Nice to meet you."

"Nice to meet you, Mr. . . ." Oh. Aneesa never told me her last name, so now I'm gape-mouthed and moronic in front of her father.

"Fahim." He half rises and extends his hand, which I shake in as manly a fashion as I can muster. "Yusuf Fahim."

"Well, nice to meet you, Mr. Fahim."

He settles back into his chair and watches me. I've made decent progress. Two of the three HDMI cables are free, an Xbox power cord is coming loose, and a white cable for something I don't recognize should be liberated soon after. "You know, when you pack these, you should fold each one up and stick it inside a toilet paper tube. Keeps them from getting all mixed up."

"I'll remember that the next time I move," he says gravely. "You're from around here, right?"

I nod. Almost done.

"I have a very serious question to ask you, Sebastian." He leans forward, elbows on knees. I freeze up, my nimble fingers leaden on the cables. I haven't even touched Aneesa. Well, other than her hand a minute ago. My throat constricts.

"Is there *anywhere* in this town to get decent Chinese?" he asks.

I laugh nervously and with relief. "Only one place. Hong Palace. It's in the same shopping center as the Narc."

"The Narc?" He raises an eyebrow. On him, it's an elegant, Spock-like movement. It's face ballet.

"Nat's Market. The grocery store. It's what we call it."

"Why?"

I have no idea. "I have no idea."

He nods, satisfied, as if my ignorance is somehow the antidote to whatever had been bothering him. "Hong Palace. Do they deliver?"

"Yeah."

"Perfect." He smiles and takes the liberated cables from me. "You'll have to tell me your secret sometime."

"Sebastian has a secret?" It's Aneesa, standing at the foot of the stairs, clutching a bottle of peroxide and a fistful of cotton balls. "I gotta hear this."

"He knows how to untangle cords," her dad tells her.

"That's boring," says Aneesa.

"Sorry," I tell her. "I don't have any secrets. I'm not interesting enough."

It doesn't hit me until later that I've lied. It felt so natural.

**Later, Aneesa and I sit on the porch, me on a comfort-**
able lounger, she on an ottoman while dabbing at my shins.

"I could do this myself."

"You'd screw it up."

"How do you know that?"

"You have a look about you."

"You know, the ground was slippery the other night. From the rain. And I just lost my balance for a second just now. It's not like I'm totally feckless."

She stops mid-dab and gazes up at me, eyes wide.

"Totally what? *What* did you just say?"

"Feckless."

Her expression goes back to normal. "Oh. I totally thought you said something else. What does that mean?"

"It means irresponsible."

"I must have missed that day of test prep." She bends to her work again, and I just sit like the mute idiot I am.

She finishes with the peroxide and slaps a Band-Aid just below my left knee. My right leg has already stopped bleeding. With a grunt of satisfied triumph, she rocks back on her heels and gestures once again like a stage magician. "Ta-da!"

"It's like you conjured that Band-Aid right onto my leg."

"I know, right?" She gathers up the damp cotton balls and scraps of paper from the bandage wrapper. "So, where were you headed in such a rush that you wiped out?"

She doesn't specify which time, not that it matters. The truth is that today I had no destination. For some reason, I just had to ride past her house and see her. But that isn't the sort of thing you can confess to a girl while she is cleaning up from nursing you back to health. Or ever.

"I was just going to this place."

"Oh, yeah. 'This place.' I know it well." An arched eyebrow is my reward and my punishment for such a lame answer.

"Seriously. Nowhere special."

She's not taking that for an answer. I don't blame her.

**The next thing I know, we're walking together along** Route 27. It's late afternoon, not yet what passes for rush hour in Brookdale. At six in the evening, 27 becomes a phalanx of slow-moving vehicles as commuters from Baltimore wend their ways home toward Cantersville. But for now, there's just the occasional car or big rig. We stick to the shoulder.

I jam my hands into my pockets because otherwise I'm afraid I'll try to hold hers. That's the sort of stupid thing I would do.

As we walk, she tells me about herself, about her family. This comes with no questions from me—I never ask people about their families or their pasts. Because then they would ask me about mine.

This is what I learn without breaking out the deerstalker: Her dad works "in finance," and Aneesa doesn't really understand exactly what he does. Her mom is an editor for a math journal at Johns Hopkins. "I don't think *she* understands what she does."

They moved here because her dad's company opened a satellite office in Lowe County, and her father was chosen to be in charge. "They're all about 'capitalizing on rural growth and white flight,'" she quotes from an overheard conversation. "Translation: All the white people are moving away from all the black and brown people, and we're being made to follow the money."

"I didn't flee from anywhere," I say lamely. "I've lived here my whole life."

"What do your parents do?"

"Mom's a translation secretary."

"What's that?"

"She speaks Spanish. And this guy who owns a company down in Finn's Landing does business all over Latin America, but he can't speak Spanish."

She clucks her tongue. "Who does business where they speak Spanish and doesn't learn Spanish?"

"Well, yeah. Mom says money buys convenience."

"I guess so."

"So Mom handles all the phone calls and correspondence and stuff."

"That's sort of cool. What about your dad?"

"Divorce. A while back." I shrug as noncommittally as I know how. "He's not really around."

"Sorry I asked."

There it is. So smooth. So adult. How did she do that? *Sorry I asked*. One moment, I'm faking a too-casual shrug to show that it doesn't bother me that she's asked about my father, covering for the fact that—surprise—it actually *does* bother me. Then, with a simple *Sorry I asked*, I'm no longer bothered. How did she do that?

"It's okay. Everyone gets divorced, right? A lot of people, at least. No big."

"Do you miss him?"

Pine. The hoot of a train's whistle. I shake my head to clear away the memories and to answer her question.

Then she asks the one question I never, ever ask anyone. No matter how curious I might be, no matter how relevant the answer might be, I never ask it, and she does, like it's nothing at all:

"Any brothers or sisters?"

# My Sister

Lola. Her name was Lola.

"No."

"Me neither," she says. "I have a bunch of friends with siblings. Half the time they seem to love it and half the time it's like they just wish they could kill them, you know?"

Oh.

Oh.

So...

"Sometimes I wonder if I'm missing out on anything," she goes on. "Do you ever wonder that?"

So...

So casually.

She said it so casually. People say it all the time, those words. *I could just kill him. I swear, if she pisses me off again, I'll kill her. Sometimes I just want to kill that guy.*

The world is filled with invisible, theoretical assassins, armed projections of our deepest ids, bearing guns loaded with wish-bullets. If you listen closely, you can hear them singing as they whiz by your head, always passing harmlessly through their intended targets.

"Do you?" she prods.

"I guess not. There's no point, really."

She pauses and turns to regard me with a thoughtfully cocked eyebrow. In my entire life, I have never noticed a person's eyebrows so much. I am only vaguely aware of my own, the sketch of light brown arches over darker brown eyes. But Aneesa's eyebrows already obsess me. They are shape-shifting punctuation for her speech, altering as necessary.

"No point," she repeats. "Yeah, that's true. It's not like our parents are going to suddenly decide to have another kid at this point, right?"

"Right."

"I never thought of it that way before. Why do I even worry about it, then? It's a moot point." She grins at me with satisfaction, with a lazy sort of joy, the kind of happiness that comes from slaying not a dragon, but rather a worrisome newt.

I grin back reflexively. Life is so much easier when you just give people what they expect.

**When we started out on our trek together, I had a** sort of blurry and indistinct goal in the back of my mind. Only partly out of conscious motivation, I was guiding us toward the old trailer. Some part of me conjured us watching it together from the cover of the trees. I wouldn't tell her what waited for me there in the future; I wouldn't tell her how my fate lurked there, patient and complacent, not needing to stalk or hunt me down, for I would come to it of my own inevitable compulsion.

I would tell her none of this, but somehow the sheer romance of the place would seep into her, and maybe I would find the strength of will to take her hand firmly, to take it like I meant it, not tentatively. And maybe I would even kiss her. A thought I'd never had before about any other girl, one that surprised and scared me and beckoned.

But in the still-bright evening sunlight, I can only hear her saying *kill them* and that overrides everything.

I find an excuse to turn us around and head home.

**I had plans for the summer. Not the sort of plans** Mom wants me to have, but plans nonetheless.

There were gaps in those plans—one big one in particular—but summer is long and I am a teenage boy with idle time. I would have worked around the gaps.

Every night for almost as long as I can remember, I go to bed and I ask the voice in my head, *Is it time yet?* And every time, the voice says, *No. Not yet.*

But then one day after spring break, Evan told me he was doing Young Leaders Camp, and a full, empty summer unfurled before me, and that night, the voice did not say *No.* That night, the voice said, *Almost. Be ready.*

And then...

And then Aneesa.

Aneesa.

Mom has the air-conditioning off to save money. At Evan's house, the AC runs full-blast, 24/7, from mid-May to mid-September.

A breeze cooler than the still air of my bedroom threads

its way through my curtains, gently elbowing them aside to waft up my bare legs as I lie in bed atop the sheets.

Tonight, I am afraid to ask the voice.

I am afraid of what it will say.

I am afraid to hear *Yes* and I am afraid to hear *No*.

**I'm not afraid to die. Not even by my own hand.**

There's an old song that says, "Suicide is painless." I'm not foolish enough to believe that's always the case, but I do know this: Suicide ends pain.

The only question is: How badly do you want to end the pain?

How badly do you *need* to?

I don't know yet. I don't have the answer. But the question always echoes, most loudly when I'm alone. I suppose some people might find that sort of psychic hectoring difficult or onerous, but I don't mind it. See, I'm in control. My future and my fate are in my hands, no one else's. I can do it or I can not. I can do it now or put it off indefinitely.

That's not scary. It's *comforting*.

Sometimes, it's the only comfort I have.

Not always, though.

The first Saturday after the end of each school year, I spend the night at Evan's. It's been this way since time immemorial, or at least the past five years. We term this day

*The Summer Kick-Off Extravaganza!* and mark the auspicious occasion by staying up all night watching old movies and concocting ever-more-disgusting arrays of junk food in juxtapositions never intended by God or Frito-Lay. One year, we dipped Cheetos in vanilla ice cream, then chased it with a hearty brew of every soft drink we could find in the house, mixed together with cherry juice and iced tea. Our flatulence that night and into the next day was truly epic to behold.

For the first few years, visiting Evan's house was like Lucy parting the furs in the wardrobe to behold the snow-filled, lamppost-lit vistas of Narnia. The sprawling manse is too small to be a mansion by any precise definition. But not by much.

Marble floors through the first level, striped with thick, densely patterned rugs. Rich mahogany handrails and accents throughout. A crystalline chandelier overhead in the foyer...and another in the dining room...and another in the great room.

(There is nothing as prosaic as a "living room" in Evan's house. Mere *living* is for lesser mortals.)

The kitchen is three times the size of mine, with two ovens, a six-burner range with a built-in grill, and a range hood that has the suction power of a jet turbine. The fridge, camouflaged into the cabinetry, measures twice as wide as my own, to say nothing of the separate, subzero freezer.

Upstairs, I've only glimpsed the rooms other than

Evan's. His brother's room. His father's home office. His mother's auxiliary closet. And I've never been to the very top floor, reserved for his parents, with their own sitting room and TV room and a bathroom that—according to Evan—has "two of everything."

Evan's room has an attached bathroom and a walk-in closet big enough for a desk and a TV.

Everything is connected, controlled by touchscreens throughout the house. Intercoms and cameras. Everything has a place and everything is in that place, not like in my house, where Mom can never decide exactly where to keep the potted spider plant or which drawer she wants to use for the big serving spoons.

Narnia. You push aside the coats and the cold air hits you and you see the soft, welcoming glow of the lamppost and you know you are far away and that at the same time you are somehow home.

That was in years past.

More recently, I've felt as though Evan's house is a museum, not a fantasyland. I've become aware of the way his mother in particular watches me whenever I'm near her. Not as though I'm a thief about to pocket the silver, but rather as though some invisible, malodorous filth clings to me and could drop off and befoul her carpets or her spotless marble floor forever.

Sometimes I wonder: Why can't they just see *me*, not

the kid who killed? But then I wonder: Is it because the two are the same?

It's bad enough to feel like an outsider. Even worse is when I wonder: Is this new behavior, or has she been like this all along and I just never noticed?

What have I been missing?

**Mom drops me off at Evan's a little after five, forc-**ing a couple of twenties into my hand "to pay for dinner." She doesn't understand that no one talks about money here. Evan orders dinner with his family's credit card and the topic never comes up. Once, a couple of years ago, I tried to broach the subject, unfolding Mom's money and placing it on the kitchen counter. I had a little speech prepared about being so grateful for their generosity and wanting to pay for that night's takeout, but before I could say anything, Evan's mom cleared her throat loudly and turned away. Evan swept the bills up like crumbs and pressed them against me as he gestured me toward the hallway and the stairs. "Let's go load up the movies, man," he said a little too brightly.

I was too young to know the word *gauche*, but I understood its meaning readily enough.

So now I ring the doorbell, Mom's money stuffed in my pocket. As I do every year, I'll sneak away to the Narc tomorrow, break the twenties, and give her a few bucks as "change." Then, a week later, I'll slip the rest of it into her wallet. She never realizes.

Evan's older brother, Richard Jr., answers the door.

"Oh," he says. "You." He says it not with disgust or outrage, but with utter nonchalance, peering past me to scan the driveway as though someone more worthy might be following right behind. "Did you see a black M-Class on your way?"

"No." I have no idea.

He grumbles and starts poking at his watch, not bothering to move aside. I press myself between him and the doorframe.

Evan comes scrambling down the left staircase into the foyer. "Sebastian! Dude!" He spares a contemptuous glance at his brother and shouts, "Hey, Tool Boy! Close the door!" receiving an almost-casual middle finger in reply.

"What a puddle of rancid douche water," Evan says, not bothering to lower his voice. "I can't wait until he's out of here."

Richard Jr. starts Yale in the fall. Once, to be polite, I asked how much it costs to go to Yale, even though I could look it up on the Internet. Evan, unthinking, told me, "It's like sixty-five per year, and it goes up each year. But they have this great program where if you prepay for the four years, you can lock it in at the freshman rate, so Dad's doing that to save money."

The surest sign that you're rich is that you don't even think about the fact that you're rich. Evan likes to act like he's above the money or disinterested in it, but he's too casual about his new iPhone, his Apple Watch Edition—which I looked up online (it cost over ten thousand dollars)—the twin to his brother's. Call him on it and he'll shrug, somewhat embarrassed, and say, "My parents want to be able to stay in touch. It's sort of practical, really."

*Practical* would have meant the same watch made out of aluminum for under four hundred. Gold is practical only in the sense of sending a message: *We can afford to buy this for our son, and since we also live in one of the safest school districts in the country—notwithstanding our son's best friend, who has a history of homicide—we're not concerned about strapping ten-grand worth of electronics and precious metals onto our child every day.*

Evan prods and guides me upstairs before his brother can snap out a lazy retort. The strip of carpeting on the stairs has been replaced since I was last here, no doubt having shown the slightest sign of wear. That's what you do in museums when the exhibits begin to look ratty—you replace them.

The carpet is so soft that I want to take off my shoes and let my toes sink into it. Later, I remind myself. I'll do this later.

On our way to Evan's room, we pass his father's office. "Evan! Come here!" his dad calls in a voice both authoritarian and excited.

The face that goes with that excitement cannot hide a frisson of disappointment when I enter the office as well.

"Ah. Of course. Hello, Sebastian."

I can't help but compare the way Evan's father says my name—as though clearing it from his throat—with the way Aneesa's father says it. Which is to say, completely normally.

Then again, Mr. Danforth *knows*. Mr. Fahim doesn't.

Mr. Danforth has a face shaped like a mangled upside-down triangle, its bottommost point—his chin—crooked and jutting out aggressively. I can almost imagine him having this done deliberately, getting plastic surgery to have his chin poking constantly at other people, reminding them that Richard Danforth Sr. is in their airspace. His hair is full and thick and too shiny. He has enormous blue eyes, frightening in their luminosity. Built like a linebacker who went paleo, he's all square shoulders and blunt forearms and wide stance. Even on the weekends, he wears slacks and a crisp button-down dress shirt, as though at any moment he'll need to throw on a jacket and tie and race off to something monumentally important and wealth-enhancing and boring.

I've never liked him. Not since the first moment we met. The feeling, I know, is mutual. Even that first time, he regarded me with suspicion, and I imagine if he could have frisked me for firearms, he would have done so.

I was seven.

But for as much as I dislike Evan's father, I have to concede that—even beyond his wealth—he has at least one trait that places him miles above my own.

Namely: He's still around.

# My Father

**Left the house when I was six.** *That* I definitely remember. I generally see him twice a year, on my birthday and on Christmas, occasions I dread. I should look forward to them; instead, I wish for them to pass as quickly as possible.

One year, a snowstorm made it impossible for him to see me on Christmas. It was my favorite Christmas ever.

My father is not wealthy, like Mr. Danforth. He is not cool and collected, like Mr. Fahim. My father bristles with energy, with regret, with time that has rotted and gone black and soft from disuse. He speaks little, asking me how school is, how my mother is, how my friends are. Sometimes he remembers Evan's name, typically referring to him as "that Evan," as though there is a plethora of Evans in my life, a vast and multifaceted panoply of them, and he is speaking only specifically of *that Evan*.

He is taller than he appears, his stooped posture shrinking him. His hair, sandy brown, a shade lighter than my own, is ragged, too long in some spots, too short in others, the right length nowhere. He favors quilted plaid shirts, worn buttoned over long underwear in the winter; open over white T-shirts in the summer, the sleeves rolled.

I've never seen him sweat.

My father speaks like someone who has never been entirely comfortable with the English language, although he is a native speaker. He halts. He backtracks. He changes tenses then returns to the original. This is when he speaks at all, which is rare. Where possible, he communicates with nods, shrugs, wordless grunts, and clucks of his tongue, expressing a bewildering range of opinions, requests, and answers without ever resorting to the spoken word.

His breath always smells of beer, but he never seems drunk.

**Mr. Danforth's office is walled in bookcases,** stocked with the sort of jacketless volumes you expect to find at library sales or in library-themed novelty restaurants. Evan has confirmed for me that the books were chosen by an interior decorator for "texture and color palette." Mr. Danforth has read none of them.

His desk is a massive slab of granite on steel scaffolding. Two large computer monitors sit atop it, and Mr. Danforth sits behind it, gesturing us over to him as he rises.

"My new toy," he says. "Just came today. Want to see it?"

Behind his desk, built into a nook carved out of one of the bookcases, is Mr. Danforth's gun rack.

Gun display is more accurate. It's a walnut-framed glass door with four rifles mounted vertically against felt. There is also a large Magnum and a smallish Colt—Evan's mom's pistol. *A girly gun*, Mr. Danforth once called it.

Mr. Danforth is the sort of man who, if we lived in Britain, would mount a horse and terrify foxes with the strength of firearms, trained hunting dogs, and the backup of four other armed men. But we live in Brookdale, in Maryland, in the United States, and so instead he fancies himself a "sportsman shooter." He spends more time oiling and cleaning his weapons than actually firing them. Writing his annual dues check to the National Rifle Association makes him feel authentic and über-Republican.

There's a fifth rifle now. Mr. Danforth unlocks the cabinet as Evan stutter-stops on the far side of his dad's desk. "Dad, uh—"

"Wait'll you see it. Absolutely beautiful."

"Dad, we—"

"Just a second..." He fiddles with the handle to the cabinet, swings it open. I catch a whiff of gun oil. Mr. Danforth lifts out the new rifle, a truly handsome piece of equipment, its stock nearly matching the grain of the cabinet itself.

"Paid extra for the French walnut," Mr. Danforth says, tapping the stock. He has the rifle aimed carefully at the ceiling, holding it so we can drink in its steely length. "Cooper M52. You know how they say, 'They don't make 'em like they used to'? Well, at Cooper, they do. This thing is gorgeous, isn't it?" He hefts it, beaming. "Isn't it beautiful? You can really do some damage with this baby."

"Dad!" Evan explodes. "I don't care. We don't care."

"What?" Mr. Danforth's lip curls in that way it does when he's been deprived or overruled. And then, as though he's wiped a patch of condensation from glass and can finally see the other side, he realizes and seems suddenly, enormously embarrassed to be standing in front of me, rhapsodizing and ejaculating over his latest death-dealing acquisition. "Oh..." he says. Nothing more. Just *Oh*.

The truth is, it doesn't matter. The truth is, it was ten years ago, and I didn't know Evan or his family then, and it's my history, not theirs. The truth is, I didn't wield a hunting rifle that day. The truth is, nothing anyone does or says can change what already happened. The truth is, guns are part of the world, of Brookdale, of life, and I can't, won't, and don't fall to pieces every time I see one. The truth is, I don't care about his guns.

The truth is *also*, though, that Evan's dad is—politely speaking—something of an asshole, and I don't like him. I don't like the way he talks through his teeth half the time. I don't like the way even his jeans—on the rare occasion he wears them—have creases in them, and you know he and his wife have never touched an iron in their lives, so who put those creases there? I don't like the gold Apple Watch he wears—matching his sons'—or the way his hair is too perfect.

So I jam my hands into my pockets and make a show of turning slightly away, a vampire repulsed by the sight of a mirror or a cross. I mumble something under my breath, not meant to be heard, going more for a tone of barely concealed anguish.

A human being would apologize. Would at least put

the rifle away. But Mr. Danforth lacks the basic human firmware required for apologies. He rooted out those files and deleted them years ago. Being rich means never having to say you're sorry. He's out of practice, and so he just stands there, gaping slightly, while Evan heaves out an exasperated huff and glares up at the ceiling.

I'm glad Mr. Danforth doesn't know how to apologize. Because if he knew how, he would, and if he did, then the only decent thing to do would be to accept it. And that lets him off the hook.

Since he can't apologize, I get to keep the emotional high ground. Studiously avoiding even a glance in his direction, I turn and—stoop-shouldered, wounded—slouch from the office without a word.

**"Sorry my dad's such an asshole,"** Evan says a little while later. We're setting up camp in his bedroom—sleeping bags on the floor, stack of Blu-rays nearby, pizza boxes still warm from the delivery guy. We'll stay up all night and gorge ourselves, beginning with prosaic chain pizza and working our way up to our combinations of grotesque snacks pilfered from the kitchen.

"It's forgotten," I say, and it pretty much is. I'm much more focused on the night to come. I need rituals, traditions like this one. Dr. Kennedy used to tell me that getting through life—especially after "a trauma like yours"—is sort of like swinging through the jungle on vines like Tarzan. (So many kids my age wouldn't have understood the reference. He would have had to reexplain, most likely with Spider-Man. But my life has consisted of a long series of unbroken strings of time alone in my room, with nothing to do but read, lest I think too much. I've been reading Burroughs and Wylie and other classic pulps since I was ten.)

*Each time you start to lose momentum*, Dr. Kennedy would say, *you look ahead to the next vine. And you jump for it, Sebastian. You don't think about it; you don't worry about it. You jump and you trust that you have the strength and the momentum to grasp that next vine.*

Every time I leap, I think this is the time my reach exceeds my grasp, this is the time my fingers will close on nothing but empty air, and I will plummet into the green and the death of the jungle.

I'm wrong every time.

So far. Anytime you swing with the apes, the plunge is only a finger's-length away.

"What ancient mess are you inflicting on me first?" Evan asks. We tossed a coin to decide who picks the first movie to watch.

"*Tron*."

He grins. "Excellent! Olivia Wilde. Oh, man."

"No, not the sequel. I mean the original. From 1982."

I might as well have told him I'm playing a recording of an old kinescope from the turn of the last century. His jaw drops. "Are you kidding me? That's pre-CGI."

"Exactly. Everything you see, someone actually *did*. A human being was there and was filmed. How cool is that?"

With a groan, he throws his hands up in the air, surrendering to my hopelessness. "I can't believe I'm gonna waste two hours of my life on something that barely even qualifies as a movie. It's more like a slideshow with motion in it."

"You've never seen it."

"I bet I'm right."

Waggling the Blu-ray case in the air, I grin at him. "It's not two hours. It's only ninety-six minutes."

"Oh, well, that's all right then. I can't believe I'm gonna let you put that diseased shit in my player. It's gonna infect it with the digital equivalent of herpes."

While we wait for the un-fast-forward-able commercials to finish, Evan asks, "What are you going to do while I'm gone this summer?"

"Oh, didn't you know? When you're out of Brookdale, the whole town packs up and goes into storage."

"Stop it."

"No, seriously. Everything just shuts down and we all go into our charging closets to receive software upgrades so that we're ready when you come back."

"You're such a smart-ass." He lazily triggers the remote when the menu comes up, and groans with mock horror. "Jesus, even the Disney logo looks ancient!"

I throw a pillow at him.

**By morning, we're reduced to monosyllables, grunt-**ing, eyes lidded, stomachs churning and gurgling with unholy concoctions conjured from the deepest recesses of our minds and Evan's fridge. We've watched nearly sixteen hours of movies, half of them from the last two years, the other half dating most recently from 1995. The sun has risen, and we're bleary-eyed and incoherent even in the confines of our own skulls.

By tradition, we have to stay awake until eight o'clock, when Evan's family has its big Sunday breakfast, imported from the 1950s and updated for modern times, Mr. Danforth at the head of the table with an iPad instead of a newspaper, Richard Jr. snarkily tossing *mals mots* from his side of the table.

Mrs. Danforth wouldn't risk her coiffure or her silk or her chemically enhanced complexion or her reputation by essaying something as prosaic as cooking, so the Danforths have a cook named Angus who comes in on weekends and for special occasions to use the million-dollar kitchen.

We eat and then it's time for me to go, my head buzzing and muzzy and all out of sorts. As I pass over the front-door threshold, it lands on me that I won't see Evan again this summer, and I suddenly feel like a small child whose mother was *right there a minute ago* but has now disappeared. I want to hug him, to cling to him, and I'm not sure why; I manage, instead, to give him a grin and a clap on the shoulder. I tell him to have fun learning how to rule the world, and he tells me he will.

In the car with Mom, it hits me anew: a summer without Evan.

I know what that means. What it *will* mean, this change in the status quo. During the school year, I always had school to distract me. Over the summers, I always had Evan.

Now, for the first time in a long time, I'll be alone with myself and with the voice from far back in my brain.

I thought I might be sad, leaving Evan this last time, knowing I'll never see him again. But instead, I'm happy. Happy that I'm leaving him with good memories. At least I accomplished that much.

And now I don't know quite what to expect.

Or maybe I do. And that's both the problem and the solution.

**A little more than a week into summer vacation, I've** managed to keep myself together. It's not time. Not yet. Still waiting for the *Yes* to come at night, waiting patiently. I have nothing but time. I have the rest of my life, literally.

I get some e-mails from Evan. I keep up with his Instagram and Tumblr. That helps.

It's not that I'm trying to forestall things, but I'm not *not* trying either. I'm exercising control. There are no rules. Nothing to say I can't try to enjoy one last week, one last month. There are books to read and movies to watch and things still worth experiencing, for now.

A job is not one of those things. I'm not going to spend my last days on earth at work. I've convinced my mother that I deserve at least a small break, a caesura, if you will, between the end of school and the beginning of my "productive endeavor," whatever that will be. She's backed off for a little while, but I know that won't last.

I can't tell Mom. Can't tell her that her insistence on my productivity doesn't matter. That her insistence that

I think about my future doesn't matter. None of that matters.

I won't be around in the future. The decision has already been made. I won't be around. Whether it's now or in a week or in a few months.

It's going to happen. Soon.

I'm almost relieved.

**One of my more annoying but—in perspective—**
mellow failings as a son is that I never, ever think to get the
mail. It just never occurs to me because mail is mostly bills
(for Mom), catalogs (for Mom), and junk mail (for Mom or
"Resident"). Mail doesn't ping my radar.

So even though I've been home all day with nothing to
do, it still falls to Mom to trek down to the end of the driveway when she gets home and fish the mail out of the box.

Today she comes in shuffling the deck of mail. I feel
my usual momentary pang of guilt for not getting the mail
earlier. And she looks up at me quizzically and asks, "Do
you know someone named 'Fahim'?"

It takes a moment to break through. "Yeah. Yeah, I do."

The envelope is small. Thank-you card sized. My
name is printed in such neat, regimented letters that for a
moment I think it's a font, but I can feel the slight, irregu-
lar indentations from the pen.

"Are you going to fondle it or are you going to open
it?" Mom asks.

I tear it open. Inside is a top-fold card with an American flag waving over script that reads, JOIN US ON THE FOURTH...

Inside, a list of what-when-where-who, with handwritten answers:

**WHAT:** FOURTH OF JULY COOKOUT
**WHEN:** FOURTH OF JULY, OF COURSE! :)
STARTING AT ONE P.M.
**WHERE:** 149 FOX TAIL DRIVE
**WHO:** THE FAHIM FAMILY

And a postscript: WHY—JUST OUR WAY OF SAYING HELLO TO OUR NEW NEIGHBORS!

And then another postscript, this one in a different ink and in a different handwriting: Whatever you do, don't ride your bike here. I want you to make it in one piece. —Aneesa

That night, I look up my name online. *Sebastian* means nothing more exotic or interesting than "from the town of Sebaste." My name is pointless.

I look up Aneesa, too, and I can't help it—I smile. It's nice.

So, yes, I'll go to the party. I'll see her again. Because...

Well, I guess just because I want to.

**I spend the days between the invite and the party** playing old video games I pirated online. They're so old that the hardware to run them hasn't been made since my parents were kids—games like *Pitfall II* and *Cosmic Ark* and *Atlantis*. You have to download the ROMs from sketchy sites, then run them with an emulator that tricks your MacBook into thinking it's a two-kilobyte Atari 2600 from 1980.

I am loathe to admit it, but this love of all things old stems from my father. Old junk from his childhood, left crammed into Lola's room, just waiting to be unearthed by a bored kid with too much time on his hands. Things from another era, an era that predated me and anything I'd ever done or imagined. They seemed to be from a better world.

And suddenly I was obsessed, haunting garage sales and estate sales and the corners of the Internet for this stuff. Like the games. I love these old games. The simplicity of them. You master them. You play them. You play until you lose. There are no complicated button combos or secret cheat codes or hidden trophies to collect. The achievement lies in lasting as long as you can, until you die.

Like life.

Last as long as you can. Hold on as long as possible. And there's no shame in losing, because everyone loses. It's just that everyone has a different score.

And the scores don't really matter after all. They disappear when you turn off the game.

**Mom says I should bring something to the party,** even though there is nothing in the invitation to indicate this. "It's polite," she says. "It's what people do." And I wonder in which class do people learn this fact about modern life? What if I missed the class, skipped over it to take chemistry or biology? What other important social ingredients does my etiquette larder lack?

"And what if I don't bother?" I ask her. "What then? Why is being a little out of step such a major felony?"

"Just do it. Don't examine it; don't dissect it."

"You'd think if they wanted me to bring something, they would say so."

"They don't want you to. But you do anyway."

"That makes no sense. Doesn't it make more sense for us to agree on something, together?"

She sighs, but it's not her annoyed sigh. It's her *my son is so goofy and so smart* sigh, the much rarer variety. But since things are going well right now, I figure maybe this is a good time to broach another topic: "Like back on the last day of school. You wanted to talk and I didn't and—"

"What do you mean?"

"When you brought up Lola and I threw up?"

Her face goes tight. "Not now."

"Look, I just wanted to…I'm just thinking that maybe we need a way to talk about it. Her. You know? Isn't it time?" Past time. I should try, I should make a real effort, before I go. Go away.

With a grimace, she flaps her hands. "You're going to be late. Don't be rude to these people."

Typical. She brings it up; I recoil. I bring it up; she recoils. We're never in sync.

And there's no arguing with parental authority. At her insistence, I bring a two-liter bottle of soda, as well as a truly gigantic bag of potato chips. Balancing the two of them while riding my bike would be impossible, so I have no choice but to accede to Aneesa's snarky wish and walk to her house.

The cookout is attended by maybe fifteen people, a decent enough total for a backyard barbecue, perhaps, but a poor representation of the neighborhood in general. Easily four hundred people live in this development. How many did the Fahims invite? I'm willing to bet most of them.

There's a red, white, and blue paper tablecloth on a picnic table piled high with bags of chips and pretzels, a card table stocked with drinks and cups (to which I add my two-liter bottle, it vanishing like a chameleon among its fellows), and a large plastic tub filled with ice and bottles of water. No beer, I notice.

The grill billows forth great gusts of fragrant smoke. I take a peek—burgers and dogs, along with delicious-smelling basted barbecue chicken skewers.

"It's Alexander the Great!" Aneesa's dad says, spying me lurking by the grill.

"I didn't cut your cords," I remind him.

"More like Theseus, then," he amends.

"Maybe more like Ariadne." Theseus navigated the labyrinth, true, but Ariadne was the one who gave him the ball of twine and the idea in the first place, so let's give her her due.

He laughs and slaps my shoulder, then wields his barbecue tongs with a flourish, gesturing to the grill. "What can I get you?"

I'm not a big eater, but it smells so good that I want one of each. "I'll try the chicken."

"Good man!" He tongs a juicy skewer onto a paper plate for me and presents it with a little bow. "Enjoy. Aneesa's around here somewhere...."

"I'll find her. Thanks, Mr. Fahim."

He pauses just a moment, then says, "Call me Joe. Everyone does."

"Okay, Mr. Fahim."

"Joe," he admonishes, shaking his tongs in faux outrage. "Joe. Right."

I step off to the side with my skewer and do what I do best: watch. Mingling has never been my strong suit. My public life began with concentrated doses of overwhelming pity ("You poor boy!") before transitioning into a bewildered scrutiny ("He's still around?") and then finally settling into a resigned acceptance of my continued existence, marked mostly by tight smiles and sharp nods and general avoidance of conversation.

Most of the people in the neighborhood ought to be able to manage at least that level of politeness. I don't need people to approach me, just as long as they don't outright avoid me. Mr. Marchetti and his wife are here, without her son, Don. Too bad. He's older than I am, but I could have at least made small talk about the comic book he publishes in the school lit journal. He's probably off somewhere with his girlfriend, a noted psychotic who has spent as much time in a mental ward as at school.

The chicken is delicious, slightly cumin-y, with a hint of garlic in the sauce. It's skewered with marinated onions and peppers, and I'm in some sort of chicken heaven, scanning the backyard for Aneesa, thinking how great it is that I can joke around with Mr. Fahim, when it hits me: The Fahims don't know about me.

About who I am and what I've done.

If I hadn't come to the party, there would be no reason

for the topic of me to come up, but with my presence, how can it not? How can someone here not mention the past to Mr. Fahim?

My gut contracts with fear and guilt. I feel like I've been getting to know Aneesa under false pretenses. Getting to know all of them. Like Mr. Fahim would never have told me to call him *Joe* if he knew what I'd done. He came here and he opened their house to me and he was nice to me and I smiled and shook his hand and lied.

The chicken has changed not at all, but my appetite for it plummets. I look around for the trash can, wondering if I can surreptitiously dump the chicken and slip away before anyone realizes I'm even here.

As I sidle into the shadow cast by the house, I notice Mr. Fahim double-checking something with a tall blond woman near the sodas. This has got to be Aneesa's mom, and there's a part of me that's surprised to see she's not in hijab. And then I wonder why I'm surprised and I wonder why I wonder so many things. Which is probably a sign that I should get away from decent people and go home.

The trash can is under the deck, on the other side of the house. I make my way there and see Aneesa, coming down the stairs, wearing a flowing skirt with a loose white shirt and a head scarf in patterned red, white, and blue. It's not quite an American flag, but it's festive, and it makes her face seem to glow.

"Chicken no good?" she asks, noticing me about to dump it into the trash.

"No, no, it's great." I make a show of eating some. "It's great." Fortunately, I don't have to lie because it really is great. It's my gut that isn't completely on the level right now.

She quirks her lips into a wry smile, but says nothing about my aborted chicken disposal. "Did you just get here?"

"Couple minutes ago."

"Where's your mom?" She peers around.

"Oh. I, uh, I didn't know she was invited."

"Of course she was invited!"

I deflect and shrug. "I don't think I can stay very long."

"I get it. Stay as long as you can."

**And the next thing I know, the sun is low along the** horizon, its light stretched deep pink like pulled tufts of cotton candy. The coals on the grill glow like spots of lava on obsidian. Aneesa has located a couple of sets of clean skewers and scrounged a bag of marshmallows, which we've speared and now drape into the heat still wafting up from the grill.

I should have left. I couldn't. Let's add one more row in Sebastian's ledger of guilt and shame.

Mr. and Mrs. Fahim (she wants me to call her Sara, and I manage to do so out loud, but not in my head) bundled the trash into large garbage bags, then gathered the paper tablecloth into its own sack and stuffed it into the big plastic toter. I should have helped. I'm useless.

"Neesa, we're headed to the fireworks," her dad says. "Sebastian, can we give you a lift?"

Before I can speak, Aneesa says, "We're just gonna stick around here, Dad."

Mr. Fahim nods slowly. "Don't go inside until the grill's out."

"I won't."

Mrs. Fahim comes to her, favoring me with a small but sincere smile. She kisses her daughter on the forehead, whispers something just below my hearing, and then Aneesa's parents are gone, leaving us alone with the marshmallows and the grill and the quiet and each other.

"Here's a secret," I tell her, before the quiet becomes too loud. "You don't have to go to the school parking lot and fight traffic to see the fireworks. Most of the good ones will come up right over the tree line." I point. "Mom and I usually sit on our back porch and watch them."

"Speaking of your mom...I thought you weren't able to stay very long."

I hope the darkening night conceals my blush. "Well, if I left now, I'd miss the marshmallows."

She groans with regret. "I. Am. So. Stuffed. I can't believe I'm contemplating this." She waggles her skewer.

"Everything was great."

"My dad's awesome on the grill. Both of my parents are good cooks."

"I can cook." I don't know why I just told her that.

"Really?"

"Well, pretty much just pizza."

She laughs. "Does your recipe involve a lot of—" She mimes tapping on a phone screen.

"No, no. I mean it. I make really good pizza." Why am I arguing with her about this?

"You'll have to prove it to me."

"How?"

"Make a pizza for me sometime."

One of the two marshmallows on my skewer is golden brown. I pluck it off and pop it in my mouth just long enough to suck off the outer carbonized shell, its burnt sweetness hot and strong on my tongue. The gooey center I respear with the skewer and put back over the heat.

She laughs. "How many times are you going to do that?"

"As many as it takes."

"We have a whole bag of marshmallows. You don't have to make them last."

It hits me: The first time I saw that toasted marshmallow trick was from my father. I shut down the memory immediately, force myself back to the present.

Aneesa has snatched one of her own marshmallows and tucked it between her lips. Her mouth is comically distended around the whitish-brown plug of sugar and her throat works for a moment. Then, slowly, the marshmallow splits down the middle and melted goo plops onto the grass at her feet. Her tongue, coated in marshmallow, wags for a moment.

She inhales the remains and laughs in good-natured frustration. "I thought that was going to look cool!"

"It looked way cool," I deadpan.

"I don't know what I expected."

"So, what did your mom whisper to you?"

Aneesa rolls her eyes. "She said, 'Remember that we trust you.' Which is totally some passive-aggressive parenting tactic they learned on the Internet. Please."

*Trust.* Does that mean they think there's a chance—

Just then, the first firework splits the sky to the east, just above the tree line. It's red and white, tracers falling out of the night sky like the despondent branches of a weeping willow.

Aneesa oohs, and an instant later, the bang comes, the explosion of the cannon that launched the firework. She startles.

"Light moves faster than sound," I tell her. "We're just barely far enough away that you can see the colors before you hear the noise."

"It's like watching a badly dubbed movie." She chuckles.

"I'm sorry. I could get my mom to take us to—"

"I *like* badly dubbed movies, you idiot." She pops her other marshmallow in her mouth and scampers up the wooden stairs to the deck. "Come on!"

There's a lounger and an old beach chair on the deck. Aneesa drags them next to each other and, still chewing her marshmallow, slips onto the lounger. She fiddles with her phone and soon the 1812 Overture is playing.

I settle into the chair, and we stare up and out together.

"Did you know he hated this piece?" she asks.

"Who, Tchaikovsky?"

"Yeah. He thought it was just a lot of noise and no art."

"That's crazy."

"We played it in band at my old school." She grins. "Is it terminally geeky if I tell you I play a mean oboe?"

"Don't they have a vaccine for that yet?"

"They should. All of those old, classical composers... Honestly, I can't stand them."

"Then why play this?"

"Because I have to admit—it just doesn't seem like fireworks without it."

I mull that over for a moment.

"Why the oboe, then?" I've never heard an oboe without one of those *old, classical composers*.

"Because the oboe is *awesome*."

"I'll take your word for it."

On overcast Fourths, all you can see of the fireworks is their pulsing glow behind the scrim of clouds with undersides gone briefly red, blue, green, and yellow in staccato bursts. But this is a clear night, and we have perfect seats to a panoply of rings and fish and spiders and peonies and all the rest, the whole gamut of fireworks in scarlet and sapphire and brilliant silver and dazzling gold. With Tchaikovsky pulsating from Aneesa's phone, we don't even notice the mismatched cannon blasts from a mile away. It's a private concert, a private light show, and my hand is achingly close to hers, resting on the arm of the chair, a gap of inches separating us.

It's the sort of time when a boy kisses a girl, I suppose.

Not that Independence Day is a romantic holiday, but there is something about a warm night, a clear sky, a full belly, and the sweet burnt smell of sugar. And maybe it's cool to touch her hand now, at least. She helped me up; she bandaged my knee. Maybe that much is all right.

And it might be. I don't know, but it might be.

But with the night sky alight with pop and crimson, I can only swallow hard, the taste of charred marshmallow skin still on my tongue, and the overture builds to the part where the cannons come in.

Bang, they say.

Bang. And bang. And bang.

I pull my hand into my lap, lest my acid touch sear her.

Bang.

Guns. Big guns.

Yes, I've fired one once.

Yes, I'll do it again.

But maybe.

I look over at Aneesa.

Maybe not just yet.

Maybe not right away.

**I don't touch her. Not until it's time for me to leave** and we fist-bump our farewell, she lightly tapping my knuckles with hers after a moment's pause.

On the walk home, I think, *I can do this. I think I can do this. I think I can make it through the summer. One last summer. That's not so bad, right?*

In bed, the voice says nothing, but its silence tells me everything.

**By the next time I pass Aneesa's house, her father** has bolted a sturdy bracket to the outer wall; an American flag flies from it. I bike by, managing not to spill myself. Third time's the charm.

The day after that, I bike by again, as though I have something to prove. I should just go up to the front door. I should just ring the bell. I should just go say hello. She invited me to the barbecue. We watched fireworks together. I should just go up and knock on the damn door.

Instead, I pedal furiously as I pass by, watching the windows for movement without seeming like I'm watching the windows.

When the time comes that I again gain entrance into the Fahim house, it comes not at Aneesa's invitation, but rather her mother's. Biking home, I pass by their house as Mrs. Fahim gets the mail. I make a mental note to myself to do this chore as soon as I am home, knowing that I will forget, and Mrs. Fahim raises her hand and smiles and says, "Hi, Sebastian!"

It's a casual wave, a polite hello to a neighbor, and certainly no excuse to stop riding, which is exactly what I do, hitting my brakes and coasting to a halt at the end of the Fahims' driveway.

"Hello, Mrs. Fahim."

"Sara."

"Right. Sara. Sorry."

I huff a little from my pedaling, and her smile falters for a moment.

"Is Aneesa expecting you?" She glances back at the house. "Because she and her father won't be back for a little while."

"Oh. Okay." As though I had plans with her.

"Would you like to come in and wait for them?"

That would be ridiculous, since Aneesa has no idea I'm here, so of course I accept.

Inside, Mrs. Fahim guides me to the kitchen. The living room, which we passed on our way, is completely unpacked, but the kitchen still has boxes on the counters and in a corner on the floor. I sit at a small table.

"Kitchens take the longest," she says, rummaging in the fridge. "Longest to pack and longest to unpack. Such a pain. I told Joe—no more moves. I'm sick of wrapping the good plates and then worrying myself sick that they don't break on the truck. Lemonade?"

"Sure. Thanks."

I thank her again when she hands me a sweating glass of it. There are actual bits of lemon floating in it, unlike the powdered stuff I make at home. It tastes clear and cool and just tart enough. I didn't realize I was thirsty until it hits my tongue. I tell myself not to gulp it and fail.

Mrs. Fahim's eyebrows arch in a way that is peculiarly and almost disturbingly Aneesa-like. It shouldn't surprise me, and yet it does, this facial tic that I have already assigned unique Aneesa status showing up on another face, albeit her mother's.

"More?" she asks.

I nod.

Turning back to the refrigerator, she says, "You're a very quiet young man. Why is that?"

"What do you mean?"

"Well, here's what I've noticed over the years: People—men, especially—are quiet for one of four reasons." She hands me the newly full glass and proceeds to tick them off on her fingers: "They're hiding something. They're afraid of something. They have nothing to say. They have too much to say. Which is it for you?"

"Maybe all four?" It's honest and it's a cop-out at the same time.

She nods. "I believe you."

"Is that good or bad?"

She shrugs. "Neither. It just *is*. When I met Yusuf, he was very, very quiet. Hardly ever spoke. My brother called him 'the Mute.'" She grins at the memory, so it's okay for me to do so as well. "And it turned out Yusuf had so much to say that he was always in turmoil, never certain *which* words to use, which ideas to advance. But even from the beginning, I could tell there was fierce emotion and intellect and passion locked up in there. So I had to marry him. I had no choice. I had to find out all of it. I had to know what was in there."

"And did you?"

She tsks and shakes her head, disappointed in me for the first time. "That takes a lifetime."

"That sort of sucks."

"Not really. Why do you think we each get a lifetime?"

I suppose the thought of it should be comforting to me, the idea that a lifetime is measured not in time, but in understanding. But how much understanding does a four-month-old have? How much did my sister comprehend? Did she know what was happening, what was about to happen, when I raised the gun?

How much did she understand in her lifetime? How much am I supposed to understand in mine?

"You're quiet again," she says.

"I'm sorry."

"Don't apologize for it. It's nothing to apologize for." And she favors me with a sensational smile that makes me want to confess everything, and maybe that would have happened, but at that moment, the front door opens and from the vestibule Mr. Fahim calls out, "We're home!"

"In here!"

98

Moments later, Aneesa is standing before me toting a paper shopping bag with twine handles, and before I can stammer out some kind of lame excuse, she grins and says, "Hey, what's up?"

"Not much. I, uh—"

"Give me a sec. I have to take this upstairs." She hoists the bag, then darts out of the room.

Mr. Fahim nods at me. "Ariadne."

"Joe."

He seems pleased that I remember this time. "Or are you going to be Theseus now?"

"Still think Ariadne doesn't get enough credit in the minotaur-slaying record books."

He chuckles and kisses his wife on the cheek. "Please tell me you didn't plan dinner. I want to try the Chinese place Ariadne here recommended."

"That's fine."

As they chat in the easy, laconic tones of a long relationship, I try to relax my face as my mind races to come up with an excuse for my visit before Aneesa returns. But by the time she's back in the kitchen, I have nothing except suggesting that I wanted to help unpack the remaining boxes, which is probably just the sort of lame move one might expect from a guy who wipes out on his bike twice in front of the same girl. Which, I realize, makes this plan one that is just crazy enough to work.

"What are we doing?" Aneesa asks, clearly excited.

*Unpacking your kitchen* would just as clearly be the wrong answer. "I thought I'd show you SAMMPark," I blurt out, without even thinking it through. It's a miracle the words come out in the right order. "It's the only park in town worth even mentioning. Actually, it might be the only park in town. I'm not even sure."

"Cool! Let me get my bike."

"Dinner in an hour," Mrs. Fahim says. "Sebastian is welcome to stay."

I'm welcome.

Welcome.

Who ever would have thought?

**Dinner is take-out from Hong Palace, of course. I've** had the sesame chicken and fried rice a thousand times, but usually on my own or with Mom, occasionally with Evan. Now I'm with an entire family, and the sensation isn't exactly like on TV shows, but it's close. We're almost a commercial for Hong Palace—all we need is a cameraman tracking around the table, occasionally zooming in for a close-up of a set of chopsticks plucking food from a plate. And a voice-over: "Hong Palace. For you. For your family. For the guy who might someday be your daughter's boyfriend, if he can ever work up the courage to bring it up."

When Mom and I eat, there's little conversation. Mealtime is a fueling stop, a necessity. The Fahims joke and laugh and ask one another for the most mundane details of their days in a way that makes it seem as though the dull moments are actually shining beacons, only covered in a thin layer of diffidence.

Mrs. Fahim grills us about our time at SAMMPark. I explain to her the story of how SAMMPark came to be, the tragedy of Susan Ann Marchetti and the man who killed her. Which isn't my best move because it sort of bums everyone out.

Mrs. Fahim breaks the awkward silence: "So, something beautiful came out of something tragic, then." It's a really nice way of looking at it, but there's nothing else to say.

Mr. Fahim clears his throat and reaches for the container of steamed rice. "You know, I was six when my parents moved us here from Turkey. And they were talking up America, of course, because I was six and afraid of moving. So they told me all these amazing things about America. But they never mentioned this." He gestures with his chopsticks to the spread before us on the table.

I feel as though I'm supposed to ask a question here, to want to know more about Turkey, about Mr. Fahim's past, but I'm at a loss. Instead, I ask Mrs. Fahim, "Where are *you* from?"

She grins. "Kansas."

Duh. I feel like an idiot. My mouth won't work. I can't speak.

Mr. Fahim rescues me. "How about you? Where are your people from originally, Ariadne?"

"Boring white places, pretty much." Completely unbidden, another Dad memory surfaces: I ask him where our family originally came from and he jerks his head to indicate outside, saying, *Over the holler a piece.*

"He's a mystery wrapped in an enigma, covered in soy sauce," Aneesa snarks, and I finally relax.

**Later, we've all decamped to the living room, where** stacks of DVDs and books remain unshelved and the walls are still bare, but the TV is hooked up and working. Partway through a reality show about home improvement—which I watch quietly and dead bored, being as polite as possible—a crawl makes us flip over to a news channel.

And suddenly we're watching a news helicopter–streamed spectacle from the town of West Janson, Iowa, where—according to the crawl and a breathless announcer—police are on the hunt for a shooter who attacked a backyard barbecue, killing at least three and wounding over a dozen others.

Mrs. Fahim whispers something to herself. Mr. Fahim stares intently at the TV, leaning forward on the sofa, elbows on knees. And Aneesa is worrying her bottom lip, which I can't stop staring at.

"Again, at this time," the announcer goes on, "police have no indication who this is or why the shooting took place. A hunting rifle was found at the scene and is believed to be one of the weapons used. Witnesses saw a figure run toward the woods nearby, and that's where police are concentrating their search. As you can see—"

"I just hope it's a white guy," Aneesa blurts out.

Her parents say nothing, but there's a tension in the room. Or maybe it's just me, the white guy.

I make excuses and leave, but Aneesa follows me out onto the porch.

"I didn't mean that personally or anything," she says.

"I know."

"It's just that, if this is a Muslim, it means…it means we have to be scared again."

Aneesa stares up to the sky, arms crossed over herself as though cold, even though the night is warm. A tear glimmers in one eye, threatening to fall. There's something in this moment that makes me bolder. Not bold enough to take her hand—I don't know if I'll ever be brave enough for that—but bold enough to think that maybe I can do something I never do: impose.

"Are you okay? Do you need…anything?" Lame. A chance to empathize, and I blow it.

"It would be nice if people stopped hating me," she says wistfully.

I've foolishly stepped into a field of land mines, any one of which could blow at the slightest bit of pressure. And my sense of direction is off, so I don't know how to back out.

Which means, I suppose, that my only option is to move ahead and hope.

"Is it hard? I mean, I know this guy—Kevin—who like suddenly became Mr. Catholic and that seems kind of difficult, but it seems like being a Muslim is a whole different kind of difficult because of, well, because of some people. And the way people feel about those people." I'm dancing around the word *terrorists* like it's the most devastating of the land mines in the field.

She purses her lips, then bites her lower one, eyes unfocused in thought.

"Never mind," I tell her. "I shouldn't have asked. I know you're not supposed to make people feel awkward and now I've done it. I'm sorry."

"Stop apologizing. Seriously. You do it all the time, for no reason. Just cut it out, okay?"

"Okay." I think about saying *I'm sorry*, totally in an ironic way, but I don't think she'd appreciate it right now.

"Look, here's the thing about being a Muslim: It's not really about us. We have one choice, one decision to make in the whole thing. We're either going to follow our faith or not. And if we decide to follow it, then…" She shrugs. "We can't help how other people react."

"But it must suck. To have people, y'know, judging you. Because of…"

"Suck or not, it doesn't make a difference. Something

sucking doesn't change what it is. What am I supposed to do? Let people's opinions of me dictate how I live my life?"

"I never thought of it that way. I guess . . . you know, growing up here, you learn not to be different. Not to stand out."

"That's sad."

"Being sad doesn't change it," I volley.

She finally relaxes and grins at me. "Truth. The Quran tells us that Allah made us all different so we could get to know one another."

"I don't get it."

"Well, if we were all the same, what would be the point in meeting anyone at all?"

"Do you believe that?"

"Honestly? I don't know. But wouldn't the world be boring if we were all the same? And wouldn't it be amazing if we were all different on purpose?"

"Yeah, I guess so."

I must still appear doleful because she grins and smacks my shoulder. "Turn your frown upside down, Sebastian— I like being me!"

"I guess I'm just worried *for* you."

She smiles broadly and squeezes my arm for just a second. "You're a good friend, Sebastian. And the good news is this: No matter how bad it's gotten for us, it's been worse for others."

"That's *good* news?"

"It's better than the alternative, isn't it?"

**It turns out the shooter is white. This is confirmed** when they find him with a broken leg roughly two miles from the scene of the shooting, still carrying his secondary weapon, a Colt pistol. He is shot once in the arm during the arrest.

I feel only relief for Aneesa, for the Fahims, at this news. No one will be assuming white people are dangerous after this.

But we are, of course. We are all dangerous, every person on this planet.

Even the children.

In bed, I relive the moments on the porch. It felt like walls came down. Like we connected. *You're a good friend*, she said.

Friend. That's a step, right? A step in the right direction?

I fall asleep on that notion.

**By the third week in July, Aneesa and I are essen-**tially inseparable. I have become, almost by accident, her guide to Brookdale, for whatever that's worth. There's nothing special or unique or even vaguely interesting about this place, but to Aneesa's eyes, it's new, and through her eyes, I discover it again. Sometimes we walk; sometimes we bike. I show her the best place for ice cream (Girelli's, behind the library building, just off the alley where Leah Muldoon was almost kidnapped by a serial killer a while back), the hidden shortcuts through town, the only decent Italian food (Sam's, on the other side of town from Hong Palace).

It's great. It's a great time. I don't even think of the voice at night. Because I crash every night, exhausted and happy, despite Mom's nagging about the summer slipping away.

Let it. If this is what it feels like to have the summer slip away, then let it.

Aneesa.

*Ah-nee-sah*.

(With apologies to Nabokov.)

It's not just that she's pretty and smart and pretty and funny and pretty, I realize. It's something more.

It's that she doesn't *know*.

She'll find out, of course. When school starts and she wanders the halls of South Brook High, she'll find out. She'll make friends, who will gossip in the bathroom, who will say, "Wait—not Sebastian *Cody*?" And she'll say, "Well, yeah. What, does he molest goats or something?" because that's her standby mock-horror, worst-case scenario.

And they won't laugh. Instead, one of them will say, "No. God, Aneesa. He killed his baby sister. Like, years ago. Shot her in her own bedroom."

And that will be the end of it.

So I enjoy it while I can. While it lasts.

I'm starting to run out of things to do with her, places to go. There's really only one left. One I've been avoiding.

But on the Friday of the last week of July, she looks at me with those bright black eyes under those high, soft, angled eyebrows, and I say, "Get your bike. Let's go." And I take her to the last place.

To my place.

**"It's a rickety old trailer,"** she says. **"So what?"**

We're in my usual observation spot among the trees as the sun burnishes the rust stains on the trailer's exterior, turning them almost bronze, almost beautiful.

I have no words to explain it to her, no words to explain what this trailer means, what it represents. What I have been planning to do within it.

When Evan left, it felt imminent and inevitable, like a storm on the horizon. Now, though, it feels no less inevitable, but somehow removed, like Christmas on the first day of fall. It's coming. It's out there. It's happening no matter what, but there's time. There's time and there's distance and there's no need to obsess over it because no matter what, the calendar pages will be torn away and the sun will set and rise, and December 25 will arrive whether you fret about it or not.

"It's just a place," I tell her. "Just a place I come. To think. To be alone."

"And you're sharing it with me?"

"Looks like."

She nods. "Thank you."

"Why are you thanking me? It's just a place."

"But it means something to you. Obviously. So thank you for sharing it."

How does she always know the right thing to say? Where does this superpower come from?

And how will I be able to say good-bye to her? I'll have to, of course. Before I take myself out of the equation for good.

Because that time is still coming. It has to. That time lives in the future, but it marches relentlessly toward the present, even as the present hurtles toward it, the two on an inevitable collision course.

Unless...Is there any chance? Any chance at all that she could overlook my past? A chance I could stay? Somehow, that's more frightening than the alternative. So much easier to imagine vanishing when that's what you know you deserve.

"Earth to Sebastian," she says, waving a hand before me. "Come in. Where did you go?"

"Nowhere. Sorry. Just thinking."

"Well, think about food. I'm starving."

"We could try—"

"No, we've been to all the good places, you said. C'mon—you owe me pizza. I'm calling you out."

"Now?"

"Now."

"I don't know if—"

She clucks her tongue.

"Are you actually making *chicken sounds*?"

She keeps clucking and tucks her fists into her armpits, flapping her elbows with all her might.

"I can't believe you're doing this."

"If you ain't bakin', you're quakin'." She drops her voice. "In fear. Quaking in fear."

"I got it." I focus, trying to reconstruct the contents of the fridge and the pantry in my mind. Do we have what I need?

"Okay," I tell her. "Quit flapping your wings and let's go."

I get a text from Mom as we get to the house, reminding me that she'll be home late tonight. Mom likes to think I don't know that her occasional "nights out" are late visits to her therapist. I don't disabuse her of the notion.

Even though my house is no smaller than Aneesa's, a part of me still feels shame at inviting her in. My home is not shabby or dirty or poorly decorated, but there is a haze of sadness and loss that permeates its atmosphere, almost tangible, just visible enough to dim the lighting. It hangs in the silent halls and hovers over the living spaces like emotional smog.

Aneesa doesn't see it, can't see it. She is numb and blind to it. She simply glances around the split-level foyer and says, "Nice."

In the kitchen, I wrestle the heavy stand mixer into position. There's no time to thaw out a dough ball from the freezer, and microwaving it never works, so I have to make the crust from scratch. Fortunately, we always have those ingredients in stock.

I prep the yeast in warm water, then tilt it into the bowl of the stand mixer. I add whole wheat flour and some herbs for a chewy, fragrant crust. The dough hook rotates, whipping along until the dough peels away from the bowl and clings to the hook.

"Now what?" Aneesa asks. She's been watching silently the whole time, sitting at the kitchen table.

"Now we have to let it rise. We have about an hour."

"So, do we just sit around and wait?"

"Nah. Let me show you my room."

As soon as I say it, I feel like a creep. But Aneesa just nods and says, "Okay."

When she crosses into my bedroom, she inhales audibly. "It's *The Land that Time Forgot….*"

"Ha-ha." I gesture her to my desk chair and she sits, then blinks at my MacBook.

"Oh. So, there *is* something from the past thirty years in here."

My room is a museum to the old, to the things I love. Movie posters for *Krull* and *Raiders of the Lost Ark*. An old CRT television hooked up to a vintage Intellivision console. A gigantic, top-loading VCR from antediluvian days. Ancient copies of *TV Guide* and *Rolling Stone* from the seventies and eighties framed on the walls. Fruits of all my garage-sale labors on display.

"You live in the past," she says in something like awe. "You figured out time travel, didn't you?"

"I just like old things."

"No kidding."

I'm not sure what I was thinking when I suggested showing her my room. The accoutrements of and from the past are comforting to me, but to Aneesa, they must be as relevant and as interesting as a typewriter.

"I thought I'd be walking into a sweaty dungeon of *Maxim* posters and video games," she says.

Video games!

I switch on the Intellivision and the TV. "Ever seen one of these?"

She swivels in the chair and looks at the control pad I hold out to her. "What planet are you from?"

"C'mon. Give it a shot."

Soon, she's giggling at the pixelated islands of *Utopia*. It's the progenitor of the god game genre, in which each player controls the resources of one of two island nations. It's really designed for two people, but no one I know will play against me, so I usually end up playing as one island or the other, reaching for higher and higher scores.

"You run this island," I tell her. "And you can plant crops and build cities and there are random storms that come through—"

"Like *Civilization* or *FarmVille*," she says. "But easier."

"Not easier. Just less complicated."

She regards me doubtfully. "Aren't they the same?"

"Play me and find out."

**I nearly forget about the rising dough in the kitchen** as we get started. After a quick session to demonstrate the basics and let Aneesa get a feel for the admittedly quirky Intellivision control pad, we launch into an actual game. At first, I have the upper hand, but playing against a real person is different from playing for my personal best and the posterity of a high score. Aneesa's an amateur at the game, but when it comes to building forts and establishing rebels on the opposing island, we're equally matched. And I've never used the PT boats, so they're not part of my plan...until Aneesa uses one to sink my fishing boat. All my usual patterns and routines crumble, and I love it.

"No, no, no!" Aneesa shrieks. A hurricane—a blocky pixelated grind of flailing white arms—descends from the upper left corner of the screen, headed straight toward her island. The last hurricane nicked my island and wiped out a factory, reducing my gold accumulation and making a new school harder to build. Now Mother Nature is bearing down on her.

I chortle in a very unsportsmanlike way and sit back to enjoy the devastation, but the hurricane pauses briefly over one of her acres of crops…and then moves off the island, vanishing off the bottom of the screen. Her crop yield doubles for the turn.

"What just happened?" she asks.

"That happens sometimes," I mutter.

She grins at me. "This is what happens when you live a virtuous life," she intones with mock solemnity.

"Bite me," I surprise myself by saying.

She clacks her teeth together loudly, and my phone alarm goes off, reminding me about the dough.

"Time to make pizza," I tell her, hopping up.

I shut off the game and head for the hallway. "Sore loser!" she shouts, following me.

"I'm nowhere near losing," I tell her, whipping the towel off the bowl of pizza dough. "You're just keeping my score down into the mere-mortal range."

The dough has risen nicely. I wash my hands as Aneesa fumes, arms crossed over her chest, then I pluck the dough from the bowl and begin kneading it.

"I can't believe you quit while I was ahead," she says.

"In your dreams."

"Next time we play, I will unequivocally kick your butt. Your island will disappear like Atlantis."

"You're welcome to try." I roll out the dough, giddy at the prospect of a *next time*. Then a thought occurs to me.

"Turn around," I tell her.

She squints at me with distrust. "Why? What are you up to?"

"I want to surprise you with this pizza. I don't want you to see the ingredients."

Her smile is sudden and open and delighted. Without another word, she turns away, and I hustle to open a can, snag spices from the cabinet, shred cheese. Soon, the pizza goes into the oven.

"Do we have time for another game?" she asks. I can't believe she actually likes it.

"The pizza only takes about ten minutes."

She peppers me with questions about school, which I'm happy to answer, but which also sink like lead into my heart. Once school starts, this all ends.

When the oven timer goes off, I paddle the pie out of the oven and place it before her. Her eyes widen and she licks her lips.

"Two more minutes," I tease. "We have to let it settle."

She groans, but waits patiently. I eventually cut the pizza and plate a slice for each of us.

"Utensils?" I ask, and she scoffs at me and sinks her teeth into her pizza.

"It's a pumpkin base with manchego cheese," I tell her, "and—"

"This is amazing!" she says, eyes alight, jaw working. "This is incredible!"

"Nah. I mean, I didn't even puree my own pumpkin. It's out of a can."

"Sebastian! This is phenomenal!" She chokes as she tries to chew, swallow, and talk all at the same time. "This is the best thing I've ever eaten in my life. Ever. You could sell this."

"What, invite people over to my house and cook for them? Yeah, right."

"No, you idiot. Like, in a restaurant. Or in stores."

"I wouldn't even know where to begin. And besides, it's not *that* good. It's just pizza."

"You minimize," she says. "That's what you do. You minimize. I say something nice about you and you contort yourself into a pretzel shape to find a way to make it meaningless."

"Some pretzels are just straight sticks."

"Add *evasive* to the list of your character flaws," she says, taking another slice. "Seriously uncool. And rude."

I start to say *I'm sorry*, but I know how she feels about that. Instead, I nod and grit my teeth and then say, "You're right."

She blinks, the slice halfway to her mouth. "I am?"

"Yeah. I minimize. I evade. You're totally right. I shouldn't do that. So, how am I going to sell this stuff?"

"Really? You're serious?"

"Aren't you?" I counter. "You're the one who put the idea in my head. You have to help me. You're honor bound. Or something." And then I hit her with the finishing blow: "Or were you lying when you said it was good enough to sell?"

"I wasn't lying!" she says hotly. "I don't lie. Especially to my friends."

"Okay. Then what's our next step? We're now Sebastian's Pies, Inc. I'm CEO and head chef. You're..."

"Taste tester and head of marketing."

"Sounds good."

So now we stare at each other and chew. "Well?" I ask after a while.

"I'm thinking," she says. "I'm *trying* to think, but this stuff is making my brain go wacky. My taste buds are commandeering my medulla oblongata. Or something."

Aneesa checks her phone to find messages from her mother. She washes her hands, thanks me for the pizza, and says, "You really could sell it," again before leaving.

As I clean up the kitchen and wrap Mom's pizza in foil, I think of the look on Aneesa's face when she first bit into the pizza, the sheer unexpectedness, the sheer joy, the delight. It's crazy to think that I've known her for not even a whole summer and today was as much fun, if not more, than I've ever had with Evan, even on our Epic Saturdays.

I don't know how to quantify the way I am around her, the person I am. When I'm with her, I feel hope. Possibility. It clings to me like a scent.

Is this what love feels like? I've never felt it before, and I've never felt *this* before, so maybe they're the same.

I could stay, maybe. For her, yes. I could stay.

*You could sell this stuff.* Not at all. Not at all. But it was fun to think about it. Fun to pretend. Fun to have someone who—for a little while—cared as much as I do.

**Later. Asleep. Beeping. Wake up. Blurry dark. Shake** head. Rub eyes. Still beeping. Clock? Can't see. Rub eyes again. Clock: half past midnight. Evan. Gotta be Evan texting. Sometimes loses track of time.

Waking up now. My phone bleats again.

Young Leaders live in a whole different time zone from We of the Proletariat.

I grab the phone and twist it right side up so that I can read the screen. The incoming text isn't from Evan; it's from Aneesa.

It's one word. I take a moment to read it a second time, to make sure I understand. But I don't understand.

Rather, I understand the word, but not why Aneesa is texting it to me at this hour.

The word is *YouTube*.

Maybe that's two words.

Me: ?

Aneesa: YouTube!

Aneesa: YouTube!!!

Aneesa: You! Tube!

Me: Quoting myself: "?"

Aneesa: YouTube is how we get sebastian's pies
started!!! You start your own channel where
you make a pizza. A different one each time.

Aneesa: And people tune in to see how

Aneesa: Like once a week. Your own cooking
channel!!!

Aneesa: And then you get advertisers and you
make a million dollars and you give half of it
to me because it was my idea

Me: U r nuts. No one wants to watch me make
pizza

Aneesa: No, U r nuts! people watch all kinds
of stuff on YouTube like the makeup girl and
unboxing videos and video gamers and stuff
like that

Aneesa: Trust me!!!

Before I respond, the chat bubble scrolls up, replaced
by a new one loaded with more emoji than I've ever seen
in one place at one time. There are multiple pizzas, hands
clasped in prayer (or perhaps begging), a white boy's face
grinning, a brown girl's face alight with surprise, more
pizza, a computer screen, and then a dollar sign followed
by the symbols for euros, British pounds, Japanese yen, and
what I can only assume to be four to five other foreign cur-
rencies, after which I believe she merely ran her fingers

across the emoji keyboard because I don't know what the symbols for—among others—poop, a haircut, a shoe, and a trumpet have to do with making pizza online.

Me: I'll think about it.

Aneesa: Nothing to think about

Me: It's late. I'm tired.

Aneesa: Dream of success!!!

I dream of nothing.

**In the morning, though, I'm convinced the late-night** text interlude was nothing more than a dream itself, until I look at my phone and scroll the evidence.

In the cold light of day, what seemed like a moderately ridiculous notion has become...

...surprisingly...

...possible.

**"No,"** Mom says when I broach the topic at breakfast. It's Saturday and she's home and I've emerged from my room for a rare morning meal with her, a token of affection that I thought might sway her to my side, but instead she favors me with a withering, exasperated look and says, again, "No."

"But, Mom—"

"No. Did you not understand the first two times?" She stabs at her omelet; it bleeds melted cheddar. "I want you to do something *productive* with your time. Not have fun with your friends goofing off online."

"It's not goofing off! It's a business!"

"On YouTube." She says *YouTube* the way a snooty gourmet says *fast food*.

"It's not just for cat videos anymore." And I have to stifle a laugh because it is quite possible I just invented YouTube's new slogan. "People make money on it."

She snorts. Someone has offered the gourmet the latest Happy Meal.

"Mom, seriously—"

"Seriously, Sebastian. I've given you a lot of leeway. If you don't come up with something this weekend, I'm going to come up with something *for* you."

Me: Now what?

Aneesa: Don't worry. I've got this

Me: Got what?

Aneesa: Trust me. Moms love me

**Aneesa shows up that afternoon, all business, wear-**ing a very conservative pair of pants and a professional-looking blazer over a button-down shirt. She has an iPad and a serious expression on her face.

"What are you up to?" I ask her as I lead her to the kitchen.

"Trust me."

Mom is waiting at the kitchen table. There's a moment of silence as they sort of size each other up. I want to laugh because it's *Aneesa* and *Mom*, not a couple of Bond villains.

"It's nice to meet you," Mom finally says, "but I'm not sure what you can tell me that Sebastian hasn't already."

Aneesa smiles smoothly. "Mrs. Cody, I'm just here to explain how having his own YouTube channel is actually pretty productive for Sebastian. I know you're skeptical, and we thought that maybe if you heard it from a neutral third party, you might be a bit more receptive."

Aneesa, it turns out, speaks excellent Adult.

"Neutral third party?" Mom says. "You're his friend."

"Yeah, but I don't really like him *that* much."

Despite herself, Mom chuckles. "Fine. Fire away." She leans back in her chair, arms folded over her chest in that way that communicates her mind has already been made up.

I nearly tell Aneesa to forget it, but she's already propped up the iPad on the table and launched her presentation. I sit silently and let her work her magic. This is her show, and besides, I have nothing to contribute other than, "I like making pizza, and Aneesa thinks this is a good idea." Both are facts already in Mom's possession.

Aneesa begins with a quick précis of YouTube itself, starting with its humble first video way back in 2005. Mom smirks a little, but politely says nothing. Then Aneesa shows a chart of YouTube's growth since 2005, titled "Eyeballs Grabbed" and featuring an animated set of blinking cartoon eyes. Mom reacts not at all, arms still folded.

Then Aneesa overlays a graph showing the decline in broadcast television viewing. It's still high, but it's dropping, while YouTube's graph seems to have no upper limit.

Mom grunts something noncommittal and her arms relax a bit.

Now Aneesa accelerates, with quick screens proving the growing financial power of YouTube. First, a graph of ad revenues, labeled "Bucks Earned" with—of course—dancing animated dollar signs, euros, pounds, yen, and more. It's more than quadrupled in the past four years....

"…and that's still not even a quarter of all video revenue," Aneesa says. "Broadcast and cable are both declining, but online is only rising. It's an accelerated growth curve, and it's not breaking anytime soon. All the momentum is with online video services, and YouTube is the biggest."

She then goes on to invoke a litany of YouTube megastars: Michelle Phan and PewDiePie and Grace Helbig and more, concluding with the holiest of holies—the Vlogbrothers.

She wraps up with a quick skim over the current online video cooking market, then shows a graph of "Projected Eyeballs and Bucks Earned" that mercifully lacks any numbers on the Y-axis. It shows rapid if reasonable growth over the next year, though, which warms my heart until I remind myself that Aneesa is making all of this up.

The last slide is a mock-up of a logo: SEBASTIAN'S PIES, in a cursive font curved upward like a smile atop a cartoon pizza crust, with two pepperoni slices for eyes to complete the smiley face.

And there's a URL at the bottom just like on a real ad or commercial: YouTube.com/sebastianspies.

"It looks like it says 'Sebastian Spies,'" Mom points out.

I groan. Yay, Mom.

**There's barely enough time for Aneesa to have got-**
ten home when she calls me.

"Well? What did she say?"

"You just left. Give her a minute to think."

"Well, what do you *think* she'll say?"

"I don't know. My mom's a pain. She's not cool like
your parents."

She huffs a too-sarcastic laugh. "My parents? Cool?
Are you *kidding* me?"

I think of Mr. Fahim's Xbox, of Mrs. Fahim's lemonade, of their easy, laconic smiles and the way they wel-
comed me into their home without a moment's hesitation.
"*I* think they're cool."

"You're welcome to them."

"Come on."

"I guess they're not *that* bad. Compared to some of my
other friends, they're okay. They try to be as cool about
things as they can. But they're always walking a line, you
know?"

"I actually don't."

"I've stumped you!" she chortles. "I've stumped the genius!"

"Are you going to celebrate or...?"

She sighs heavily. "I don't expect you to get it. I mean, it's a mixed marriage, right? Which is cool, but sometimes there's a tension. Because Dad is religious and Mom isn't. And I feel like I have to balance them, even though they don't put that kind of pressure on me. And we...never mind."

There are two ways of saying *never mind*. One way means *never mind*. The other means *I want to keep talking about this, but it's getting to me and I'm not sure I should, but if you encourage me, maybe I'll keep going.*

Aneesa's employing the latter.

"Keep going," I tell her, and she does.

"It's tough to talk about this stuff. But I guess if I don't, no one will learn. You wouldn't get it. You don't know how lucky you are. Both your parents were born here and *their* parents and *their* parents, and you don't have this stress of 'We're not really welcome here.' And 'We have to honor our past, but also be a part of the place where we live.' And sometimes that seems impossible."

Replace *honor* with *live with* and I almost understand.

"I didn't mean to vent like that," she says quietly. "It's just that we're the Muslims no one thinks exist and we're right here and it's frustrating sometimes." There's a long

133

silence filled with expectation, and I realize I haven't said anything.

"I didn't mean to go all quiet," I tell her. "I'm sorry."

She chuckles. "You're apologizing again! All is right with the world."

That night, Mom knocks on my door. She doesn't actually come in, but rather leans against the frame. I realize that I can't remember the last time she came into my room.

I'm on the bed, flipping through a copy of *Replay*, a book from 1986 that I reread at least once a year. It's about a man who dies and wakes up to discover he's in his own past, able to live his life again. I consider it the me-equivalent of the Bible—most likely full of nonsense, but comforting to fantasize about.

"You can do it," Mom says.

It takes me a moment to connect her words to Sebastian's Pies.

"Are you serious?"

"I think you should change the URL or the name of the . . . it's not really a company, is it?"

"I don't think so."

"Well, you should change it. But go ahead, Sebastian. Do it." She grimaces for just a moment. "But you really need to commit to this. This isn't just a hobby now, or something you do when you're hungry or bored. You need to commit."

"Got it."

She nods. "It's good to see you smiling."

I hadn't realized I was. I widen it a little, just to see how it feels. Then I grab my phone to text Aneesa, but an idea occurs to me. Before Mom can get away, I make her stand in the doorway, and I record her saying, "Hello, Aneesa. That was a very persuasive presentation. I hope you and Sebastian enjoy your little venture." She's a good sport about it and says it with more enthusiasm than I believe she actually feels.

It takes a couple of minutes for the video to shoot over to Aneesa, but then I get back a flurry of emoji, one of which is a pair of kissing lips, and I think, *Really? Maybe?*

And that night, I don't bother asking the voice if it's time yet. Because for the first time that I can remember, I don't want to know.

**We figure we'll do a video each week, which seems** manageable.

Right. The first week on YouTube is something of a disaster.

Our first pizza—a pesto sauce with homemade whole wheat crust infused with basil—is a massive success. Our first video, less so.

Other than shooting short blurts of video to send to friends and family, neither Aneesa nor I have ever recorded anything of any substantial length. We quickly realize that we need to learn how to edit, not merely for length, but also for pacing and clarity. Aneesa finds an online tutorial (on YouTube, of course) about editing video and stays up late figuring it out.

By mutual agreement, we change the name of our channel to "Sebastian Cooks," both to avoid the spying connotation and to make it sound more active, more urgent. I also insist that we not show my face—there's no point to it. The focus is supposed to be on the pizza, so we show only my hands as I go about prepping and cooking. Besides, this way, whenever I fumble in my improvisational recitation of my process, it's easy to lay in a new soundtrack in editing.

Aneesa reluctantly agrees and takes long, lingering shots of the ingredients, as well as dropping in the occasional slo-mo of my hands kneading the dough.

"It's called 'food porn' for a reason," she points out.

Week two's video is much better. Our second pizza is a cornmeal crust with pepper jack, grilled jalapeños, and onions; a real mouth-burner. In one week, Aneesa has mastered the camera and the software, and the video looks great. We post it and get precisely zero views, despite sending out the link on Twitter, Instagram, and Facebook.

"We need velocity," Aneesa says. We're sprawled on the floor of her living room, laptop open before us to the Sebastian Cooks page. It's been a couple of days since we posted the second video, and a whole lot of nothing has transpired. She idly taps REFRESH over and over, hoping to see the view count increment. No luck. "John and Hank Green posted videos every single day when they started Brotherhood 2.0."

"I can do every day," I tell her.

She shakes her head. "There are only so many combinations of ingredients. I don't want you to burn through your repertoire before we get any traction."

"It's *pizza*. There's an infinite number of things you can do with it. Don't worry about that. But look—school starts in, like, a month. We'll have to cut back on this then. Now's the time to go nuts, right? So let's do a pizza a day."

She clucks her tongue, deep in thought. Her brows come together like two waves cresting at each other, or like the top half of a heart.

"Will your mom be okay with pizza every day?"

I shrug. Mom's paying for the ingredients, so technically I guess she has to okay it. "If you look at it a certain way, this was all her idea. She's the one who wanted me to do something with my time this summer. Besides, who could get sick of pizza?"

And so we begin cranking out pizzas and videos every day. Despite my confidence in the unlimited variety of pizza permutations, I am—inside—a bit worried that my pizza-crafting mojo might falter or wane as time goes on. In order to pace myself, I alternate inventive—white pizza with roasted artichokes, sun-dried tomatoes, and Bella Vita cheese on parsley-infused crust—with faithful standards—mozzarella and pepperoni with margherita, the pepperonis cut into wedge shapes to make them stand out from the usual.

I narrate each step as I go along, and Aneesa inserts herself and her phone into my workspace to catch the close-up details. We still have some difficulties to overcome—I'm not used to someone in my space while I cook, and she isn't sure how to capture everything without interfering. But by our fifth video—a white pizza with sliced summer squash, arugula, chiles, and fontina cheese over a basic Neapolitan crust—we have a system down that works for us, with Aneesa devising an on-the-fly series of taps on my side to indicate if I should slow down, speed up, or do something again.

Our follower and viewer counts begin to grow the tiniest bit, but nothing beyond low double digits. Each night, I sink into bed and into a confusion of emotions. Baking new pizzas every day is tiring but energizing at the same time. Working with Aneesa is intoxicating (or so I assume, having never been intoxicated), but the lack of attention paid to Sebastian Cooks frustrates me. If I'm going to do this, I want to do it well. And I want people to acknowledge that.

*It's all just a distraction*, says the voice one night.

It catches me off guard. I'd almost forgotten the voice. Is it speaking the truth? Is this all just a distraction? A pleasant diversion before the gruesome finale, what they call in opera the *Grand Guignol*?

Just a distraction.

But a good one.

**At the beginning of the third week of our endeavor,** Aneesa comes over early, a very grave, worried expression on her face.

"What's wrong?" I guide her into the living room.

"Don't be mad," she says, plopping her laptop down on the coffee table.

"I'm not mad."

"Don't *get* mad, is what I mean."

"Why would I get mad?"

"Promise."

She's so serious and so earnest that I have to throat-clear a chuckle into oblivion. "I won't get mad."

With a half-unconvinced sigh, she opens the laptop and plays a video. It takes me a moment to realize that it's our most recent episode, in which I assembled an admittedly too-bitter pizza topped with radicchio. It takes me another moment to realize that there's no sound, but before I can tell her to turn up the volume, it happens.

A voice.

The original sound is gone, muted, in favor of a new vocal track. A voice speaking in a calm, measured, yet somehow breathless tone all at the same time, like a golf announcer. A voice with the slightest trace of an accent that could be British. Maybe. Or maybe not.

Finally, I realize—it's Aneesa.

She's dubbed over the entire episode, using some strange variant of her own voice. It changes the nature of the show—suddenly, it's not some kid telling you how to make a pizza, but rather an admiring onlooker who encourages others to peek in and see something wonderful happening. The whole operation transmogrifies from a simple process story to an appreciation of the labor and the love and the art.

"...now watch as Chef Sebastian dices the onion," faux-Aneesa purrs with satisfaction. She calls me *Chef Sebastian* throughout the episode. "I really respect such skill with a knife, don't you? So deceptively simple. And now...into the pan, to sauté! I wish you could be here to smell the olive oil and the onion...."

Silent and amazed, I find myself caught up in the moment. Even though those are my hands on the screen, and I know exactly what they are and will soon be doing, I can't help but admire the craft and the precision on display. I've watched my own videos before, of course, but always with my own voice narrating, always acutely aware that *This is me. This is me.* Now, though, it's an entirely different experience.

The video ends and Aneesa turns to look at me, worrying her lower lip. "Well? What do you think? I just thought"—she rushes on—"that maybe a different kind of narration might, I don't know, change things up a little, but if you hate it, we don't—"

"I love it."

"You do?" Her expression goes from worry to delight at light-speed, with no intervening steps. Even if I didn't love the new narration, I would fall in love with it right at this moment from the sheer joy my approval brings to her face.

"It's just what we needed. It takes the focus away from the guy making the pizza and puts it *on* the pizza."

"But it also makes you sort of mysterious!" she says excitedly. "It's like, 'Who is this mysterious Chef Sebastian?' And that will get people thinking and talking and watching. I can go back and reedit the old ones. There aren't that many of them, and no one's really watched them yet."

I nod, not even hearing her now because something else has occurred to me. It popped into my head when I said *It takes the focus away from the guy making the pizza and puts it* on *the pizza.*

"There's one more thing we need," I tell her. "The most important thing."

"What's that?"

I grab her hand, too preoccupied to be surprised by my own boldness, and drag her off to the kitchen.

**Later, we watch a rough cut of that day's new epi-**sode together. Aneesa narrates in her almost-British golf-announcer voice as I assemble a crabmeat-and-roasted-artichoke pizza atop a super-thin crust, with cheddar and alfredo sauce. It's mouthwatering, and I cannot imagine anyone watching this—with the exception of those allergic to shellfish and super-observant Jews—who would not want to press themselves through the screen and take a bite.

Which is what's been missing. As the pizza comes out of the oven, Aneesa zooms in for a super close-up. My hands disappear and then reappear wielding a pizza cutter. I deftly (if I do say so myself) bisect the pie on the diameter twice at right angles, then halve one of the quarters.

Then Aneesa's hand comes into frame, snagging a slice by the crust and lifting it. With only a minimal amount of camera jiggle, she manages to follow her hand, turning the camera on herself as she guides the slice to her mouth and takes a huge bite.

And chews.

Eyes rolling in bliss.

"That is *so* good!" she exclaims, and takes another bite as we...

Fade to black.

"It really was," she says now, toying with the crust of her last slice. Between the two of us, we inhaled the entire pizza while watching the rough cut. Usually we save a slice or two for Mom. Not today.

"This is what was missing." I can't help myself; I grin. "When I heard you narrating, like you were enjoying the whole process, that's when I realized. We need a person. It's about the pizza, but we need to show someone enjoying it."

And it's about her, too, I don't say. About that look on her face the first time she took a bite of that pumpkin-and-manchego pizza. That look that thrilled me. If it thrills our audience half as much...

Who am I kidding? I don't care about the audience. Just watching her.

Nodding, she types at the keyboard for a moment. Our page's keywords are updated to include "girl eats pizza." She pauses, thinks, then revises to "Muslim girl eats pizza."

"Why?"

She shrugs. "I don't know. Just sounds better. So, I

guess it's pizza every day for me from now on. Man, I'm going to get fatter than fat doing this."

"Well—"

She chuckles. "It's worth it."

We touch pizza crusts like clinking champagne glasses.

**And I wake up later that night,** my breath hot and rapid. A part of me wishes it were just acid reflux from the pizza, but I know it's not. It was the dream. A dream of my father.

Sitting up in the dark, I can't remember the details, but it felt like him, sounded like him, tasted like him. He was there, in the dream, and I don't know why, but I know that I can't go back to sleep.

I dress without turning on the light. Two of the stairs to the foyer landing creak, but I avoid them. The front door's hinges need to be oiled, so I sneak out through the basement instead.

No bicycle tonight; I want to take my time. It takes twice as long as usual, but eventually I arrive at my observation point among the trees, watching the still and silent trailer.

What am I doing? With the pizza stuff, with Aneesa? How have I lost sight of what's important, what matters? The plan I've had for years now, the one that was coming, marching relentlessly toward me.

Is it because I'm happy? Am I happy? I don't even know. Like love, it's too foreign for me to translate. And does it even matter what I feel now, in the present? Does that override the past? Can it?

Do I deserve to be happy?

No. Of course not.

I lost sight, yes, but I haven't forgotten. I promise I haven't. I'm still going to do it. Yes. I am. I just need some more time. I'm not stalling. It's only a matter of time. A matter of when, not if.

I promise.

**The daily schedule and the new gimmick of Aneesa** narrating and eating the pizza work. We burn through double digits on our subscriber count in the first week of the new, improved videos, then enter into triple digits. I at last inform Evan of my summer project, via text, and he responds with enthusiastic emoji and the news that "all the guys here" are enjoying the videos.

Aneesa has one more trick up her sleeve—a theme song. It's bouncy and bright without being cloying or annoying. It's absolutely perfect.

"Sounds like more than just an oboe," I tell her. "What talents are you hiding from me?"

I could swear she actually blushes. "Just the oboe is me. The rest of it I did in GarageBand."

We don't necessarily go viral, but we catch the digital sniffles. Soon, we hit one thousand subscribers, and our videos begin picking up multiple viewings per person.

Along with the good comes, of course, the bad.

The usual welter of ridiculous comments and nonsense—virtual catcalls, some disturbing racist barbs, misogynist snark—begins to clutter our comment section. I want to pull the plug on them, but Aneesa shrugs it off, pointing out that some of our commenters are acting in our defense against the trolls.

"Remember," she says, "we're all different for a reason."

"I'm supposed to learn something from these submoronic jackasses?"

We're at her house, sitting at the kitchen table, waiting for our latest episode to finish rendering on her laptop. Her parents are at work and *we trust you*, so we have the run of the place. I still have half a glass of Mrs. Fahim's good lemonade, but I'm too hot for it to cool me off.

"The comments are aimed at me, not you," she points out. "Don't get pissed."

"That's *why* I'm pissed! I don't care what anyone says about me."

She *hmph*s. "I don't know if I should be flattered that you care so much or offended that you think I can't take care of myself."

"Aneesa..."

"Think, Sebastian. What's really bothering you? Do you really think I need a big strong man to save me?"

"Hey!" I stand up, jostling the lemonade. "It's not about that. That's not us."

*Us.* What is *us*?

"Then sit down," she says very calmly, gesturing to my chair, "and stop worrying. I'll tell you when it's too much for me, and we'll deal with it then."

"How?"

"I have no idea. Fortunately, I don't need one yet."

I'm still angry. On her behalf. At her, too. I don't think she needs to be rescued. But when you see your friend—or someone you think and hope might someday be more—abused, you do what you can to stop it. Who doesn't do that? What kind of person *doesn't do that*?

"You're still upset." She sighs.

"No, I'm not."

"You haven't sat back down."

I sit. I sulk. I'm obvious.

"You act like this is the worst thing that could happen to me. The worst thing that *has* happened to me."

"One guy said he has some meat that definitely isn't halal for you to put in your mouth!"

She laughs. "And isn't that the stupidest thing you've ever heard? That guy doesn't know who I am or where I live or even my name. I don't care what he says. I've heard worse. In person."

It takes me nearly a minute to work up the courage, a minute spent with my chin on the table, tracing curves in the condensation on my glass of lemonade. "What's the worst thing you've heard?"

She tuts and waves the question away like a mosquito. "Boring. Boring, boring, boring. What other people do and say. People who are irrelevant. Ask me something that matters, Sebastian. Like, what's the worst thing *I've* ever done to someone else."

"I don't want to know."

She leans over the table and slides the glass away so that it's no longer between us. Our eyes lock. "Because you're afraid it'll change what you think of me?"

"No. I just don't care."

"Friendship without conditions or strings?" She grins. "Wow, that's really open-minded of you."

"No. I just don't have a litmus test for my friends, is all."

That stops her cold. She rises and comes around to my side of the table, looming over me, sizing me up. I lean back in my chair and look up at her. "What?"

"You're really smart," she says. "And really mature."

"Thanks, Mom."

She punches my shoulder. We've come a long way from those early days when she wouldn't shake my hand. "Stop it. I'm being serious. It's a compliment, loser."

"Putting the words *compliment* and *loser* next to each other makes for some nice cognitive dissonance."

"See? That's what I'm talking about. Who talks like that? Seriously. I mean, write it on your blog, sure. But who actually speaks out loud like that without rehearsing?"

"Sorry."

"There you go, apologizing again! I'm seriously in awe, jackass. I'm not dissing you. I'm marveling at you."

I've never been marveled at before. At least, not in my field of vision.

"You don't ask your friends about the worst thing they've ever done because you know deep down they'd disappoint you, and you're too noble to let that happen. That's what it is."

"It totally isn't."

"Then what's the worst thing *you've* ever done?"

Freezing water in my lower intestine. My guts lurch and my muscles tense. I mumble something indistinct and only vaguely words.

"I'll go first," she says, cheerfully blazing ahead. "When I was ten, I knew my best friend liked this guy that I also liked. And I stole her diary and ripped out the page where she wrote that and left it in his locker so he would see it. She was mortified and I had broken her trust and it was pretty awful."

"I guess so."

"Do you hate me now?"

"Nah."

"See?" She smiles dimples. "No big! Now you. Go ahead."

"I don't want to." But.

"Come on. I just bared my soul to you. The least you can do is return the favor."

But I suddenly do want to. I don't know why. I don't understand it. I'm not even sniffing around the edges of understanding it, but suddenly I want more than anything in the world to tell her. Because she thinks I think she needs help. Because she mocked me for wanting to help. Because I want to show her she's not the only one who's been pissed on by the world.

She's regarding me with those quirked lips, those arched eyebrows. I want to tell her because I realize now that it's true: I love her and I need her to know, and if I don't say it now, I'll never say it, and it has to come from me.

"When I was four years old, I shot and killed my baby sister."

Her face freezes. Her expression doesn't change, but somehow manages to become different from mere seconds ago. It's the eyes, of course. The lips and cheeks and eyebrows stay the same, but the eyes themselves go dark, closed while still open.

With great difficulty, she swallows. "That is *not* funny." Her voice, a whisper that grows without warning into a near-shout. "That is *not* funny! What kind of person jokes about that?"

"It's not a joke, Aneesa. I swear."

"Stop lying. That's disgusting," she says, and turns away, wrapping her arms around herself.

"Get out your phone," I tell her, "and Google *Brookdale*, *Maryland*, *toddler*, *sister*, and *shoots*."

Her back to me, I can perceive only the tightening and hunching of her shoulders, the pause of her breath. She fumbles for her phone. I watch as her fingers dance across the glass, conjuring letters, words, my past, my sins.

A pause. She holds the phone at reading distance in a hand that begins to tremble.

"*Inna lillahi wa inna ilayhi raji'un,*" she whispers, and when she turns to face me, tears have cut trails down her cheeks. They glimmer there like the paths of falling stars.

"This was you?" Holding out the phone. I flinch at the headline: *Boy, 4, Shoots, Kills Infant Sister.*

It's kryptonite. It's garlic and a crucifix. Wolfsbane. I rise from the chair, fall back a step, then another, its glow toxic and cold and burning me.

"Don't make me. Don't make me read—"

"I'm sorry."

From her for once. The satisfaction is hot gravel down my throat, settling in my stomach.

My name isn't in the article, of course. Nor is my mother's, my father's, Lola's. The victim was a minor; the shooter was a minor. The media protects us. Too late, the media protects us.

"This is really you?" she whispers, the phone turned back to her now, her face alight in cold blue, like reflections off a pool at night.

"Yes. It's really me."

"Fox Tail Drive," she mutters, then looks up sharply, staring open-mouthed over the top of her phone. "That's here. That's where we live. It happened in the house you're in now? You didn't move?"

You try selling a house where a baby was killed, I want to say. But I can't bring myself to.

"Oh, Sebastian." The words strangle her. I worry she can't breathe, but she keeps talking. "Sebastian. I don't even...I can't even...Why didn't you tell me? Why didn't you say something?"

"So you could hate me sooner?" I snap.

"No, you asshole!" The words explode out of her, and she actually throws her phone down on the table in outrage, finally looking up at me. Tears stream down her face. "So that I could *be here* for you!"

"You *are* here."

"I think..." She trails off, and then, without warning, without a word, she hugs me, her arms around. It's the last thing I expect and the first thing I want, and somehow it feels all wrong. I stand there, stiff and unyielding, mute, and we're both silent and then—after millennia—I melt against her, neither of us speaking, neither of us moving, both of us barely breathing.

The temptation is to cry. To let my tears join hers. To commit the final sin of weakness and allow myself a relief and a release I simultaneously crave and have forfeit. But I haven't cried to my mother and I haven't cried to my therapist. I won't cry to her, to Aneesa. I won't. I bite the inside of my cheek; I focus on the familiar, delicious pain.

And this is the moment to kiss her, but this is the moment never, ever to kiss her. Because to kiss her now is to seal it with pain and shame, and nothing grows well or true or right in that blend of fertilizer. So I need to, but I can't, and I stand steady and I hope that I did the right thing, that whatever my motivations, it was the right thing to do, that I'm not just trying to spread out the burden or entice her with pity.

She pulls back. Her gaze flickers between cold and hot, whirlwinds of flaming hail in her eyes.

"What happened?" she whispers, and I say nothing because, what is there to say?

"The story says it was an accident," she goes on. "What happened?"

"I don't know. I was four. I don't remember."

"Do you remember *anything*?"

"No."

The quiet surrounds us; we are suffused by it and by the past.

With a shake of her head, she comes to the present. "So, wait. You don't remember. So, how…? How did…One day someone just…*mentioned* that you'd done this?"

"No. No, not like that. I was just four. But I've always…I've always been *aware* that I did it."

"I don't understand."

"Like, do you remember learning to walk?" I don't let her answer. "Of course not. But you know you learned at some point because you can walk and you've always been able to walk."

She mulls this over for a moment. "It's like that?"

"It's a little like that."

This seems to satisfy her, if satisfaction has any place here, at this time.

"What did you say before? 'In a lily way...?'"

"*Inna lillahi wa inna ilayhi raji'un*," she says. I'll never get it right. "It just means...It's something we say when something bad happens."

"Something bad happened a long time ago. Not now."

"I don't even know what to say. I don't. 'I'm sorry' feels useless."

"You can't treat me any differently. You can't do that." I mean to sound insistent and confident, but pleading has crept into my voice. I'm begging, not demanding. "It's not fair to treat me differently. You were the only person in this town who didn't know. I didn't have to tell you."

"But—"

"No. And don't tell your parents. They like me."

"You think this would make them *not* like you?"

I think of Evan's parents. "Well."

"My parents think you're great, Sebastian. My dad practically *quotes* you, like you're Shakespeare or something. You think he tells every random kid he meets to call him by his first name? That's not typical. He really likes you."

I try not to not let my shock and my pleasure show, but I know my face betrays me. It almost always does. "Let's keep it that way. Right now they see *me*, not…not what I did."

She nods. For the first time, her hijab slips the slightest bit, and I catch sight of hair so deep brown it's black. Then she tucks it away smoothly, so quickly that it's gone in the instant I realize I've seen it.

**The next time I go to Aneesa's house, Mr. Fahim** makes a joke about Saint Sebastian. Nothing has changed. She hasn't told them.

Good.

**We're in Aneesa's living room two days later,** watching the pilot episode of *Max Headroom* on my laptop. She has taken my words seriously and not treated me any differently. A part of me imagined that learning about my past would either repel her or bring her closer to me, but she's acting as though she hasn't learned something horrific.

Which is what I wanted.

Right?

She's sprawled prone on the sofa, chin resting on a pillow. I'm leaning against the sofa, sitting on the floor. We recorded at her house today, which her parents are cool with since this isn't just messing around—it's "a productive endeavor." And now we each have a slice of pumpkin-manchego pizza. Until this afternoon, we'd somehow missed making a video of what Aneesa calls "our inaugural pizza." Mrs. Fahim—Sara, I mean—pronounced it "truly amazing" when we offered her a slice. I'm officially expanding my clientele.

"I don't get this," Aneesa complains for the fifth time since starting the show. "Why is everything so grainy? Why does he look like that? Those are the worst computer graphics ever."

"It's from the 1980s. And Max Headroom isn't computer-generated. They actually used makeup and prosthetics on the actor to make him look like something computer-generated."

"It's not working," she says drily. "So, wait—why did that other guy's head explode?"

"Because of the blipverts."

"The blipverts."

"Right."

"Which are…"

"Hypercondensed, subliminal commercials that get beamed directly into your head. They're killing people by accident, but no one—"

My phone chooses this moment to bleat for attention. Aneesa's does, too. I pause the video, and we both check our phones.

"We did it!" she shouts an instant before I realize why.

We've both received an e-mail from YouTube with our latest stats—we've gone over ten thousand subscribers. By exactly one. We have attained the palindromic status of 10,001 subscribers.

"We did it!" she shouts again.

It's a false milestone—nothing special happens at 10,000 subscribers—but it's one we've been anticipating as our subscriber base has grown. More subscribers mean, ideally, more views. And more views mean that Aneesa's plan to monetize the channel might actually work.

Almost in spite of myself, I'm obeying Mom's command to be productive.

"I can't believe this many people want to watch you eat pizza."

"They're watching you make it first, dummy. Don't you read the comments?"

"Not anymore." It's Rule One of survival on the Internet.

"Well, the ones who aren't jackasses are mostly complimenting you on your mad skills. One guy says he's a chef at a place in Des Moines and would totally offer you a job."

I snort. "Ah, yes. Des Moines, Iowa. Renowned as the pizza capital of the world."

She bats me with a throw pillow, then does it again for good measure. "It's a compliment, you idiot! Learn to accept it!"

I deflect another blow from the pillow. We're both breathing hard and now would be a good time, but, no. Why? Because *always* "but, no," that's why.

And because sometimes I catch her looking at me with pity. Sometimes, I catch her looking sad. And I get it, I really do, but I can't let it happen now, under those circumstances. Not out of pity.

It's not fair, what she could do to me, or what I could do to her.

"We need another gimmick," she says for no particular reason.

"Hitting me with pillows, perhaps?"

"No. Too easy." Punctuating her point, she craftily bonks me atop my head with a stealth swing I don't see coming. "I'm thinking of something outside the box a little."

"Outside the pizza box, you mean?"

She groans and feints with the pillow. I flinch. "Who told you you were funny? Who lied to you so viciously? What," she goes on, "can we do that's different?"

"I still have ideas for some recipes—"

"That's not what I mean. Maybe we should try something other than pizza."

"Pizza's our schtick," I argue. "And besides, I don't really know how to make much of anything else."

"I just want to keep our numbers growing."

"I know."

"I mean, pretend we *are* a restaurant." She leans back on the sofa, arms crossed at her belly, hands clasped. She stares at the ceiling. "Say we're the best pizza restaurant in the world. People love us. We're packed, lunch and dinner. Our head chef obstinately refuses to cook anything but pizza—"

"*Scrupulously* refuses."

"—so we can't branch out that way. What do we do?"

Gloriously, I know. I know in an instant, I have the answer.

"Breakfast," I tell her.

She sits up and blinks at me. "Breakfast pizza?"

"Yep. Breakfast pizza. You said our restaurant is full for lunch and dinner. So we do breakfast."

Her eyes light up. She leans closer to me. "Not just breakfast. The whole deal."

"We already do lunch and dinner, though." Now I'm confused.

"We do it all at once." She hops off the sofa and grabs her laptop. "We do it next week. Right before school starts. An all-day extravaganza. To juice our numbers so that when we drop to a weekly schedule for the school year, we have some padding to lose people. You'll make pizza for breakfast, lunch, and dinner."

"And dessert," I tell her. I have to top her.

"Dessert?" she asks. Then: "Dessert!" she chortles and begins pounding at the keyboard.

Evan: Hey theres a guy here whos dad has
some yt channel w like a billion followers
want me to send him your link?

Me: OK

**I type "OK," but inside I experience a whirlwind.**

I never really anticipated the pizza channel accomplishing anything. I never imagined it as an achievement. At first, it was nothing more than a convenient distraction, a way to keep Mom from nagging, an excuse to spend time with Aneesa.

And now it's like something's been born. Unintentionally, sure, but good, in its own way.

But holding me back?

Maybe?

I don't know anymore.

I don't know anything.

I want to keep baking pizza.

I want to go away.

I want to figure out how Aneesa feels about me.

I want to end it all.

I want.

I want.

I want.

I want too much and I don't know what I want at all.

It used to be so easy, so clear.

I stay up late. I have to figure out how to make a pizza crust out of cookie dough.

**On the last Wednesday before school starts, we do** what Aneesa has billed in messages to our subscribers and on social media as "The All-Day Pizza Extravaganza."

At 8:30, Mom leaves for work. At 8:45, Aneesa arrives. "Are we ready?"

"Yeah."

First up is breakfast pizza: a layered soft taco shell crust with a black bean sauce topped with scrambled eggs, salsa verde, and crumbled blue corn tortillas. The blue verges to brown in the heat of the oven, so the impact of the blue chips against the yellow eggs and green salsa doesn't work the way I wanted it to. But when Aneesa takes her on-screen mouthful, she pronounces it "super-amazing," so I consider the experiment a success.

We enjoy the pizza, toasting with virgin mimosas, congratulating ourselves on a job well done. By the time we've eaten, then edited and posted the video, it's time to start lunch.

I had considered a peanut-butter-and-jelly pizza—somehow—to tie into classic lunch fare. But I couldn't wrap my brain around the hows of it. And, honestly, there's no way to improve on the sandwich.

Instead, I reach back to another lunchtime favorite from my childhood—tuna.

Beginning with a whole-wheat crust, I slather on a layer of mild chipotle sauce, then top it with wilted spinach, coarsely grated cheddar, and chunks cut from a gorgeously grilled tuna steak. The result, according to Aneesa, is "the best tuna melt you unlucky sods out there in YouTube land have never tasted."

Edited. Posted. Move on to dinner. No rest, not today.

Unable to help ourselves, we devour each pizza in its entirety.

I prep dinner, which is a super-thin whole-wheat crust with a light oil sparingly applied, really just painted on. I top this with thinly sliced pears and sautéed onions, then add crumbled goat cheese. The goat cheese bubbles and browns as Aneesa breathlessly narrates, her camera zooming in on the glass oven door. I'm sweating so much that I think I might pass out. I reveal the day's third pie.

"I think I hate pizza now," Aneesa jokes. "I'm going to excuse myself to the bathroom and stick my finger down my throat."

"Vomiting up the meal is considered an insult to the chef."

"Then I'll make it my middle finger, to be doubly insulting."

We each eat a tiny wedge. It's so delicious that we agree

we each want more, but it's been too much pizza for one day, despite the desires of our taste buds.

"I can't believe I survived this," she moans, slumped over the table.

"You haven't survived anything yet," I remind her. From the fridge, I produce the cookie crust I spent yesterday baking so that it would be ready for this moment.

"For the first time in the history of me," she says, "I don't want dessert."

"Well, our website says 'Muslim girl eats pizza.' You got another Muslim girl lurking around?"

She thumps her head against the table. "I hate myself. I hate myself. I hate myself."

"But you're gonna love dessert."

"I hate dessert. I hate dessert. I hate dessert."

Mom gets home just as I'm prepping for the dessert pizza. She notices the pear-and-goat-cheese pie, the still-on oven, and arches an eyebrow.

"We left it for you," I tell her. She grimaces, but once she takes her first bite, her expression softens.

"You already cooked. Why is the oven still on?"

"Something new." I show her the cookie crust and her eyes light up.

"Really?"

"Really."

Mom glances at Aneesa, who is trying to remain upright in her chair. "Was this your idea?"

"Sort of. It's all his execution, though."

"Let's see how it goes, then."

The pizza stone is still hot after a day's use, but I can't simply lay my cookie crust on it—it would absorb the savory oils from the other pizzas and ruin its own sweetness. So I commit a sin against the culinary gods of pizza and lay parchment paper on the stone, moving quickly lest I burn myself.

Paper in place, I prep the crust, topping it with a layer of pasty fudge, then a drizzle of caramel, followed by sliced banana, a sprinkle of chopped walnuts, and a ribbon of more fudge.

Into the oven it goes, for just a few minutes. Just long enough to make the fudge gooey and to slightly caramelize the banana slices.

When I remove it from the oven—with a motion I feel I've repeated a thousand times today—Mom actually gasps and applauds. Aneesa, despite herself, grins broadly and joins in the applause.

"Not done yet," I warn them.

I spend a couple of minutes hand-whipping some whipped cream and float stiff arches of it over the pizza. When I'm done, it looks like shredded clouds drifting over a delicious, edible field.

I cut small slices, bearing in mind how sick and tired of pizza Aneesa and I are.

We each eat two of them.

Later, I lie in bed in the early stages of a sugar coma, combined with a general food coma. I am brain dead on carbohydrates and complex sugars, unable to move, capable only of staring up at the ceiling. Evan's bedroom ceiling hosts a complicated, meticulous glow-in-the-dark decal replica of the night sky, with a particular focus on the Big Dipper. Mine features a pebbly popcorn texture and a small crescent of water damage in one corner from when a pipe in the ceiling froze and cracked one winter.

A knock at the door. As per usual, Mom stands in the doorway, not entering.

"Good job today, Sebastian."

I struggle into a sitting position. "With what?"

"With everything."

"Oh."

She sighs and smiles at me. "I'm really proud of you. I told you to do something productive with your summer, and you have. I check your page, you know."

"Please tell me you don't read the comments."

She grins. "I'm old, not stupid. Look, I've been watching your views climb. You're in some pretty impressive territory."

"It's nothing compared to—"

"Stop it." She holds out a hand, like a crossing guard of language making certain no stray words are hit by an oncoming linguistic semitruck. "Stop it, Sebastian. Stop putting yourself down. You've built something. You've applied yourself. And I want you to know that I'm so proud of you."

She bites her lip. "Look, I know we don't always...I know we don't always talk...about the things we need to talk about. And I'm sorry for that. I just..."

I can't stand to hear her apologize to me. And it's been a day. I'm stuffed and logy. "It's okay, Mom."

She beckons. Despite the pizza I've stuffed into my gut over the course of the day, I swing my legs out of bed, give myself a moment to catch my breath, and then go to her.

She takes my face in her hands and gazes into my eyes. There is something in there—words, I think—that she struggles with. I don't know if she's struggling to withhold them or to say them. But after a too-long moment, nothing issues forth. She tilts my head down, kisses my forehead gently, and whispers, "Good night."

**And with that, we've recorded our last daily epi-**sode for the time being. "Our big season finale," Aneesa calls it.

We still have the rest of the week. I take Aneesa on a tour of the last few places worth visiting in Brookdale. And then, on a whim on Friday night, just as the sun is setting, I take her to Lola.

**There are four graveyards in Brookdale that I know** of. My sister rests in the one behind the South Brook Episcopal Church.

"My parents used to go to church every week," I tell Aneesa as we look down at the grave. "They stopped."

Aneesa seems ill at ease here. I can't tell if it's the rampant Christianity or the so-brief span of time etched for all eternity into Lola's headstone. February to June of the same year. Even though I know—even though I *did it*—I still double-check every time I visit, recalculating in my head. It seems so wrong, so *off* to have such an abbreviated life chiseled into granite. But it's right, of course. It's right and wrong. LOLA MARIE CODY and two dates and the words LOVED FOR A LIFETIME.

Aneesa toys with the tail of her hijab, her face unreadable. "If they stopped going, why did they bury her here?" There's a hitch—not quite a hiccup—between *they* and *bury*. The word isn't difficult—it's the thought. A tiny body, barely a body at all, six feet below where we stand, in a coffin the size of a dollhouse. Unthinkable. And too easily imaginable.

"My mom wanted a place, I guess. A place to come to. I think...I think maybe by making it a separate place, she could separate it in her mind as well. She could leave it here and not carry it with her all the time."

"And what about your dad?"

I flinch at the mention of him. "He just always went along with whatever Mom wanted. For a while. And then he wouldn't go along with anything. And they argued over everything. *Everything*. Like, what kind of toothpaste to buy. Screaming matches over junk like that."

She sighs. "What about you? Does it help for you to have it here? Does it help you not carry it?"

"I told you—I don't remember any of it. I don't have anything to leave here."

"If you *could* remember—" she begins.

"Please don't finish that sentence. I've heard it my whole life." *If you could remember, you could get past it.*

It's warm, but she shivers. "Do you want to pray? I can pray with you, if you want."

"No, that's okay. I don't know any prayers."

"Prayers are just talking to God, is all. There's no right or wrong way."

I shake my head. "No. I just like being quiet here."

She nods. We stand in silence. After a little while, she takes my hand.

Less than I want. More than I deserve.

**Should have kissed her.**

Why didn't I kiss her?

She took my hand. She made the move. Why didn't I kiss her?

Because I'm going away.

Am I? Am I still?

I think. I think I need to. I think.

Should have kissed her.

Evan: You there?

Me: Where?

Evan: lol I'm home now. tired. hang tomorrow?

Me: OK

Aneesa: Awake?

Evan: Where/when?

Me: Yeah

Me: sammpark 2?

Aneesa: Can I call or too late?

Evan: k

Me: Sure

Aneesa: Ring ring! lol

"I have an awesome idea," Aneesa says when I answer.

"I'm sure." I can hear her tapping a pen against the lid of her laptop, a tic that expresses itself whenever she consults our YouTube analytics page. "What's wrong with our numbers?"

"Nothing's *wrong* with them. I just want to keep it that way. We got a nice bump from the extravaganza, but I'm worried that once we're only pizza-ing on the weekends, we'll lose all of our momentum. I think we need one more big push right before school. Something that will get people's notice and keep them interested. Sort of a 'wow, who knows what they'll do next!' kind of thing. Then we can coast a little."

Heaving out a sigh, I try to keep a note of whining out of my voice. "I made four pizzas in one day. What else can I do?"

"Livestream."

"What?"

"Do it live. No recording. No editing. No second takes. We stream it live."

I have always been confident in my skills, and the summer has honed them and made me even more confident. That's what making something like a couple dozen different pizzas in a row will do for you. Still, the idea of a livestream just seems to beg for disaster. "I don't know. What's the point? It's the same thing as a regular episode, just live. There's nothing exciting about it."

"It's the unknown factor. People tune in because they think anything could happen."

"Listen to yourself. It's *pizza*, not surgery. What, do they think I'm going to set myself on fire or burn the house down?"

"I don't know what they think. I don't care. I just want them to watch. Maybe…" Her voice bursts into a musical giggle for a moment. "Oh, man, I've got it! We make it a challenge! People love stuff like that. We make it a thing where people tell you—live—what ingredients to use and you have to come up with a pizza."

"Ugh. I don't know.… That doesn't sound like fun."

"You don't have to do it *every* time, or all the time. Just every now and then. It'll get lots of attention drawn to you. Lots of views and hits and comments. We could start pulling in some advertising and make money on this. That would pretty amazing, right?"

"Do we have to let them tell me what to make? I sort of

have my own ideas about what makes a good pizza. It all sounds a little too *Chopped* to me."

She sighs noisily into my ear. "What if we just make it like a Q&A? We'll let people ask questions. I mean, a lot of our comments are questions about making pizza. You could answer them live."

"A lot of our comments are sexist and racist and, and, and—"

"The word you're looking for is *Islamophobic*."

"Right. That."

"But mixed in there are genuine questions."

Now it's my turn to sigh. "You want to open the floor to the idiots who troll you in the comments? For every person who asks about kneading dough or preheating a pizza stone, you're gonna get ten jackasses promising to stuff you like a grape leaf."

"That's an image I'd like to scrub from my brain."

"I'm trying to impress upon you how—"

"Once again, Sebastian, I don't need you to protect me. You worry about the cooking—let me worry about the comment trolls."

I surrender. Sometimes I feel like that's all I do with her.

I meet Evan at SAMMPark in our usual spot, near the statue of Susan Ann Marchetti. He looks the same, dressed too casually in jeans and a T-shirt that individually cost more than everything I'm wearing, yet designed to look as raggedy as my own clothes. Wish someone could explain that to me.

"How was Illuminati Camp?" I ask him, clasping his hand.

"Man, I missed you and not understanding half of what you say." He reels me in for a one-armed bro-hug, which I reciprocate. It's good to see him again. Texts and e-mails and Instagrams aren't the same.

We break our clinch, grinning, and walk into the park. "Half of what I say? On your best day, you get maybe twenty, twenty-five percent of my references. The Illuminati are these guys who are rumored to secretly rule the world. Have since, like, olden times—"

"Oh, *those* guys." He waves at the air. "Sure, sure. Dad has them over for poker on the third Saturday of every month."

"How was it?"

He groans, annoyed that his deflection hasn't ricocheted the question into the upper stratosphere, where he doesn't have to deal with it. "Truth? It sucked. Boring as hell. God, I hate rich kids."

"Self-loathing is a strange trait in you."

A grunt and half-smile. "Tell me about your summer."

"You saw it. It was online." But I go ahead and give him the basic history of it all, how it started, how it progressed.

He eyes me warily, regarding me with the sort of penetrating vision and comprehension only a longtime friend can muster and project. "There's more to it than pizza. You're into this girl, aren't you?"

By now we've walked deeper into the park, not really paying attention to our path. We've played here since we were kids; we know this place better than we know our backyards. I manage a halfhearted shrug, an unspoken nondenial.

"Have you been, like, *with* a girl all summer long and you didn't tell me?" he demands, half in excitement, half in outrage. "Dude!"

We close in on the fountain at the center of the park, ringed by six benches, each with a dedication plaque set into it. I can recite them all from memory.

"Not so loud," I reprimand, and sit on TO THE MEMORY OF ALLEN HALEY.

Evan drops a coin into the fountain. The town actually prefers that people not do that, and there is a sign posted to that effect, but Evan does it every time we come here anyway. He leans against the fountain's rampart and crosses his arms over his chest. "You have a girlfriend. Wild."

I shake my head. "Nah. Not yet." And then I proceed to fill him in on all things Aneesa-related that are not specifically pizza-related. Our Fourth of July together. Our sharing of old movies and TV shows (at my suggestion, but she enjoys them). The way she took my hand.

"I'm just waiting for the perfect moment," I tell him. "To make my move. You know?"

Evan worries his upper lip with his teeth, then shrugs. "Look, I don't know how to say this, but...you've been friend-zoned, man."

"Have not." There is more heat in my voice than I intend. How would he know? He doesn't have a girlfriend. And he's never met Aneesa.

"Hey, you would know better than me." He shrugs again. "I'm just saying—you wait too long, they start to think you're not interested. They stick you in the friend-zone. You know?"

Evan is my best friend and Evan is rich and Evan is smart, but Evan doesn't know everything. He doesn't know Aneesa.

"Just...never mind about her, okay?"

"Okay," he says with equanimity. Equanimity comes easy to Evan. He's never disturbed by anything. "What classes did you pull this semester?"

Our schedules are e-mailed to us a week before school starts, along with recommended reading lists and, if the teacher is on the ball, a class syllabus. We dig into our pockets for our phones so that we can see which classes we'll have together.

We've managed to land in the same Algebra II class, as well as Chemistry I. We've also managed to sync up on World History I, Economics, and lunch.

"Who do you have for English?" I ask.

Evan grins, folds his hands over his heart, and gazes with gratitude toward the heavens. "Miss Powell. There *is* a God, Sebastian, and He has bestowed upon me Miss Powell."

Miss Powell is not just the hottest teacher at South Brook High—it's entirely possible she is the hottest teacher in the world. Her hotness is bolstered by the fact that she dresses like a nineteen-year-old and aims her flirting at the whole class at the same time, probably barely skirting the edge of laws designed to keep teachers and students from clawing each other's clothes off.

"Wow," I say, for there's nothing else to add.

"Wow, indeed. Wow, indeed. How about you?"

I look down at my schedule, even though I have it memorized. I've got Ms. Benitez for English. More specifically, for a class called "Accelerated Composition and Structure."

"Tough pull." Evan winces. "My brother had Benitez for ACAS. She's a hard-ass."

"I can handle it."

"That's a senior-level class. Why are you taking it early?"

"To get it out of the way, I guess." The truth is, I'm not sure *why* I signed up for ACAS so early. I didn't even think I'd get in as a sophomore. I've always taken the toughest classes, the most advanced ones. There's never been a question. Otherwise, I get bored. So I just figured, *Why not?* Maybe I should have asked *why* instead.

"It'll work out," I tell Evan.

He comes closer and stares at me for an uncomfortable moment. "Your summer was good?"

"Well, yeah." I'm a little flustered by his sudden intensity. "I told you."

"Okay. You just seem different."

"Different good or different bad?"

He takes long enough to answer that I know he's actually considering. "I can't tell," he confesses. "I guess that's why I had to ask."

The plan is to record episodes once a week on the weekends during the school year, but for Aneesa's live-stream idea, we do it the evening before school starts. Mom helps us out since Aneesa needs to be able to ask me questions and hold the microphone to me—we don't have a clip-on, and I can't cook and hold a microphone at the same time. We show Mom the best angles to use, and she manages to keep out of our way while still keeping everything in frame.

Aneesa has an iPad with an app where the questions come in. She shadows me, trying to keep from distracting me too much while also staying out of Mom's shot. We manage to keep things moving, and the few times we collide, it's funny rather than hazardous. We laugh a lot, and Mom laughs, too, even though we tell her to stay quiet.

By the end, I've answered about twenty questions from live viewers, and I take my first on-screen bite of pizza. A basic whole-wheat crust topped with a bianca sauce, wilted spinach, shrimp, and shredded Romano cheese.

"That's amazing," Aneesa says as she chews on her slice.

"It's not bad," I concede.

"Talent and humility!" Aneesa crows at the camera. "You've witnessed it here, folks! Keep watching—it's school time, but there's still more to come!"

That night, after kissing my forehead, Mom says, "I really like her."

"So do I, Mom."

**First day of school, following a summer I couldn't** have expected or anticipated. It happened so fast that I don't even know what to think of it. And now I have to decide: Sit with Evan or with Aneesa on the bus?

Evan makes it easy for me—he's on the bus already and sits with another kid, on the aisle. Aneesa and I slip into the empty seat across from him. I make introductions. They nod politely at each other.

"Strange to see you without pizza," Evan teases gently.

Aneesa flashes her teeth at him and shoots back, "I thought Sebastian invented you."

They laugh at each other, and I release a breath I can't remember holding in the first place.

**First period is ACAS. I am the lone sophomore in a** room full of seniors. I find a seat in the back, near the window, and think of Evan, no doubt already in a glazed-eyes state of lust over Miss Powell's sartorial selections *du jour*.

Ms. Benitez is wearing a severe dress with creases sharp enough to slice Romano cheese. Her chin comes to a threatening point, recalling to mind Evan's dad. I'm beginning to think I made a mistake signing up for this class.

I tune in as she's ranting about the word *nice*. Ms. Benitez is apparently a general in a holy war against this word. She seeks nothing less than total annihilation.

"Eliminate this word from your vocabularies," she insists. "Not just in this class, but in all your classes, in your lives. This is not a word that describes, that evokes, that conjures. It's useless. It's meaningless," she rails, "and you all use it constantly. 'He's nice. She's nice. How was the dance? It was nice.'"

As though possessed by the need to emphasize her point, she scrawls the word on the whiteboard in ten-inch-high letters and then X's through it savagely.

"*Nice* is the white bread of the English language adjective breadbox. It's tasteless, bland, and forgettable. When you speak, when you write," she says with the air of a fire-and-brimstone preacher, "I want you to do it *multigrain*."

I've changed my mind. I was totally right to take this class. Evan can have super-hot Miss Powell. I think I'm in love with Ms. Benitez.

I catch up with Aneesa between classes. "How's your first day?"

"Good. Good." I'm glad she didn't say *nice*, a word that hitherto had seemed innocuous but is now ragingly offensive to my linguistic palette. She's distracted, juggling her books and a sheet of paper. I help out with a spare hand.

"Thanks," she says. "Where is 'Tinselly 2'? I have a class there, like, two minutes ago."

"Oh, that's inside the band room. You have to go through the band room, and there's a little hallway, and Tinselly 2 is back there."

"How am I supposed to know that? On the map, it looks like—"

"I'll take you," I tell her. I march ahead confidently, and since I still have her books, she has no choice but to follow.

"Other than the mysterious labyrinth within which lies Tinselly 2, how's it going?"

She shrugs, a little more calm now that her destination

is no longer a mystery. "Fine. I guess. A little annoyed at how white bread all the reading is."

*Nice is the white bread of the English language adjective breadbox.*

"What do you mean?"

"It's all this old stuff," she complains.

"Hey, I like old stuff!"

"Oh, so you don't mind a steady diet of old white men?" The challenge in her voice is unmistakable. There is a right answer and a wrong answer to this question.

And, I suppose, an honest answer.

"I never thought about it that way," I admit. "I just always try to extract some meaning from what's in front of me. Whatever it is."

She considers this. "And I guess I never thought of it *that* way."

"Someone once told me there's a reason we're all different."

"Anyone ever tell you you're a smart-ass, too?" she says drolly. "Band room! Excellent. Thank you, kind sir." She mock-curtseys, swipes her books, and disappears inside.

I make a mad dash for my next class.

**It usually takes a few days for me to adjust to the** new school year, and this year is no different. By Thursday of the first week, I've figured out when I can listen, when I can tune out. The syllabus for Ms. Benitez's class is rigorous, but not surprising, so I fade from class for a moment to consider the upcoming weekend and the first filming of a Chef Sebastian video concurrent with the school year. I want to craft something unexpected. I want, to use Ms. Benitez's parlance, to bake *multigrain*. To prove to people—and to myself—that being back at school has not dulled my culinary wits.

I'm so focused on possible recipes that I nearly miss Ms. Benitez's pronouncement.

"I've been thinking about this all week," she says, "and I've decided to add something to the syllabus."

A groan erupts around the room. The workload in ACAS is onerous enough without adding more.

She holds up a hand to forestall complaints, her mouth set in a grim, resolute line. "Enough. This is simply one more assignment. I'm confident you can all handle it. You'll have the entire semester to work on it, so you can fit it in between other assignments.

"I used to make this particular assignment mandatory," she goes on, "but I stopped a few years ago. I've been thinking recently, though, that most of you could benefit from it." She stares unnervingly at us, somehow making it seem as though she's staring at each of us individually. "You're not babies anymore. You're not children. You are young men and women, and I expect you to act like young men and women. Which means thinking of your futures. College or whatever your plans are. If you're in *this* class, though, I can't imagine your future plans *don't* include college.

"No matter what you do in life, you'll need to think critically. And you'll also need to think *self*-critically. To examine your own actions and look for ways to improve. And to get into college, you're going to need to write about yourselves.

"So. The assignment is this: You will write an essay about a significant event in your life, and what you would or would not change about it. The essay is not due until the end of the semester, but I expect you to be thinking about it and working on it throughout. You'll want to touch base with me at least a couple of times through the semester to make sure you're on the right path."

And she goes on and on, and then she drops it and starts teaching, but I hear only white noise and see only red.

*A significant event in your life, and what you would or would not change about it.*

*A significant event in your life.*

*And what you would*

*Or would not*

*Change about it.*

Are you fucking kidding me?

How about: not pulled the fucking trigger?

**When the bell rings, I abandon English like it's the** *Titanic,* racing from there as though the room were filling rapidly with water and piranha. I stumble through the halls toward my locker, the sounds around me muted, the sights blurred.

She can't mean—

She can't want me to—

But what else is there? What else *is* there?

It's got to be a mistake. An oversight. She's thinking about the class, not each student, right?

I can't do it. I can't. There's no way. This is insane. How am I supposed to—

At the lockers, Evan is holding forth with a group of his friends. They're his friends, not mine, though I spend time with them almost by default. I like precisely none of them, and right now all I want is to get the books for my next class and escape to the mind-numbing pleasantry of my wood shop elective. I can't tolerate Rich Kid Babble. Not usually. And especially not now, my mind churning like tornado clouds over Ms. Benitez's assignment.

"Sebastian!" Evan says, as though I am a weary traveler he's not seen at this tavern in many a fortnight. "How's Benitez treating you?"

"Not well," I confess, and spin my combination lock.

"Sebastian?" says Mark Vesentine. We've met before; we've hung out before. But he has to act as though he's never heard of me. "Sebastian. Oh, yeah, I've seen you online. You're the guy who makes those pizza videos. Yo, that shit is *tight*."

Rich White Kid Trying to Be Black—*double* can't tolerate.

"What's it like making pizza for Jihadi Jane?"

There's an oceanic roar that starts in my ears and grows to envelop me. It picks me up like a child's doll, buoys me dizzyingly, turns me, aims me. Before I realize it's happening, I spin around, grab Mark by the shoulders, and slam him against the lockers. My own voice is strangled and drowning but still audible to my ears as I shout, "Shut your fucking mouth! Shut your fucking mouth!"

Hands grapple me, pull me away. There is a glimmer of bravado in Mark's eyes, swamped by shock and fear. I struggle against the hands on me. They're Evan's. He's tugging me away from Mark.

"Come on, man, you know that shit ain't cool."

I don't know if this is directed at me or at Mark. I don't care, either.

"Just making a joke," says Mark, miffed. "So fucking sensitive. Jesus Christ. Or should I say Mohammed?"

Evan's grip on me tightens again to hold me back, but it's not necessary. I've burned through the adrenaline rush.

"You're a fucking asshole," I tell Mark, slamming my locker shut.

"At least I never shot anyone," he fires back. There's a communal gasp, but I don't even turn to look at him, marching off instead.

"Someone should have shot *you* in your fucking crib," I toss back at him.

**On the bus ride home, I deliberately sit away from** Evan. I'm not sure if I'm angry at him for stopping me from pummeling Mark or for being Mark's friend in the first place. I just know that I'm still angry, that the rage smolders under there. Mark's comments about Aneesa, about the shooting—they are the tinder. Ms. Benitez's assignment is the spark.

Aneesa tries to engage me in conversation. I do my best to be polite, but she can tell something is wrong.

I can't tell if I'm angry or grateful that she doesn't ask what.

At home, I throw my backpack into the corner, hurl my body onto the bed. Time passes. I'm not sure how much. I can't imagine how to write this essay for Ms. Benitez. I can't imagine what she was thinking telling me to write it in the first place.

My phone buzzes, and I flip it over to see the screen.

Aneesa: DON'T LOOK AT THE COMMENTS!

Aneesa: Coming over RIGHT NOW

**Time disappears. It vanishes and slides. It's gone** slippery and slick, threading through my fingers like oil.

Aneesa is standing in front of me. I don't know how she got into my bedroom. I don't remember the doorbell, and Mom isn't home yet.

It feels as though ten centuries have passed, but it must have only been fifteen minutes.

Her face is twisted in concern, her eyebrows cresting above her eyes, crashing on either side of the crease stitched by worry above the bridge of her nose.

"You looked, didn't you?"

Yes. Yes, I did. I looked at the comments.

Specifically, at the fifteenth comment posted to the archive of our livestream.

Before then, all anyone knew about me was my first name and what my hands looked like. I never really thought about it before. I was anonymous without even trying.

A few days ago, for the first time, they saw my face.

The fifteenth comment.

"hey I know this kid. he goes to my school and he KILLED HIS BABY SISTER. don't take my word for it—" and a link. I didn't click on the link. I don't need to click on the link. I know where it goes.

There are many, many comments after the fifteenth. They're all basically the same.

"Sebastian," she says.

"I am so sorry," she says.

I can't think of anything to say. Except: "Our subscriber count is down."

"Don't worry about that now."

"We're losing subscribers," I say.

She puts her arms around me. "Don't look. Don't read."

It starts to happen—I feel myself melt against her. My eyes flutter closed.

Her lips against my hair, pressing against my scalp.

"I'm so sorry." Her breath. The sound of it.

I wallow in her.

She absorbs me. Arms around me. Cradling me.

I pull back, just enough. Lean up. Crane my neck.

There's a question in her eyes and on her lips. I blunt it with my own lips, pressing them to hers, doing it at last, at last doing it.

I'm kissing Aneesa. My body dissolves into a burst of color.

And she pulls away, pushing at me at the same time.

"What are you doing?" she asks gently.

I don't know how to answer. Isn't it obvious?

"You can't do that," she says.

Fumbling for words, still coalescing from my explosion into color, I manage to say, "Is it a Muslim thing?"

"That's not…" She backs away a little bit. "It's a *me* thing. I don't feel that way about you."

The words are standard English, arrayed in appropriate syntax, but they make no sense. This is *Aneesa*. She's spent the summer with me. Introduced me to her family. Spent Fourth of July watching fireworks with me on her deck. Held my hand. *Held my hand*.

"But you do," I tell her stupidly.

"I don't. I'm sorry. I'm really sorry. I didn't know—I had no idea you felt this way. I'm sorry."

And the worst thing is this: She really *is* sorry. I can read her; I've spent the summer reading her. She really, truly is sorry.

It's true and impossible.

"What the hell, Aneesa? You held my *hand*—"

"I was trying to comfort you!"

"—and you spent your whole damn summer with me, making *pizza*. What the hell is that about?" My voice hasn't risen, but it's become tighter, tauter.

"I did that because you're my friend and because it was *fun*, you idiot!" She's gone brittle. There's a tension along her jaw I've never seen before. "I *liked* it! It's possible for me to like doing something without being in love with you!"

"You led me on—"

"No. I never said anything. I never said we were anything but friends. Not once. I can't help what you—"

"Why did you let me think you liked me?" It comes out a whine with bristles accrued to it.

"I didn't do anything except be your friend," she says quietly. "I've always been honest with you."

"Yeah, *now*."

"No, always," she says firmly. "But, yeah, *especially* now. I could have lied to you. It would have been a lot easier. I could have told you I was gay. Or blamed my dad, or my religion. I could have said that I had a boyfriend back in Baltimore. Because guys will listen when you tell them you belong to someone else. Like, you'll respect some made-up guy, but not me. I thought you were different. I trusted you. I told you the truth."

"Get out," I tell her, my voice dull. Lifeless.

"Look, we should—"

So now I scream it. I feel cords standing out in my neck, cords I've never felt before. I feel a sharp, almost painful tug deep in my throat.

Aneesa leaves.

She leaves.

She leaves me alone.

Which is right.

Which is how it should be.

I read every last comment. A part of me is amazed at how many different ways people can misspell *murderer.*

The roar of the ocean is back. The buzz in my ears intensifies. I close my bedroom door and turn out the light and crawl under the covers. The comment thread flickers and scrolls on the backs of my eyelids.

*Murderer.*

I don't want to go to school in the morning, but Mom will ask questions, so I force myself out of bed and into clothes and onto the bus, where I sit in the front, away from Evan and Aneesa.

Evan approaches me when we get off. "Dude, are you still pissed about yesterday?"

"I'm fine. I just had to finish my algebra homework."

Aneesa does not approach me.

I walk through school, certain that everyone knows, that everyone has seen the video and read the comments. They've all known, of course, forever. They've all known. It's not like it's a secret. But it's always been unspoken. And now someone has spoken it. Someone here, in my school.

It could be anyone. Safely ensconced within the anonymity of a YouTube screen name, it could be anyone around me, even a teacher cloaked in the rhythms of online teenspeak.

At the end of ACAS, as everyone else gathers up their books, I approach Ms. Benitez at her desk. At least there's one thing I can fix. "Can I talk to you for a minute?"

"'May I speak with you?'" She doesn't allow herself a moment's distraction or distance from the paper she's reading.

Of course. Idiot. "May I speak with you?"

She looks up at me and smiles. "Of course you may, Sebastian."

I'm not sure where to begin, so I just plunge in. "It's about the essay assignment. The semester-long one. I know you want us to learn to do something like this for college applications, but I'm a sophomore. I'm wondering if there's a substitute assignment I could do. Or maybe some kind of extra credit to compensate."

She narrows her eyes.

"I'm not saying it's too difficult," I hasten to add. "It's just that it...it's difficult...in other ways."

Her expression is flat, unreadable. Blank paper; blank screen. "Sebastian, you volunteered for this class. You requested it. No one made you take it."

I regroup. I take a breath. Not a deep one, just *a* breath. Just a quick moment to gather myself.

"Look, you know who I am. You know about my past."

Her expression flickers momentarily, a soft expression of grief and compassion before returning to stone. I'm used to this. It happens all the time around me, this unconscious projection of sorrow.

"You don't have to write about *that*," she says. And then dead stop. She thought it would be easier to say than it was. She thought if she said *that* and didn't use specific words referring to specific events that she could do it and not feel awkward, but she's realized that the awkward is a part of it, no matter what words you use.

"What else important has happened to me? What else can compare?"

The class is nearly empty now, a few stragglers lingering at the door. The room is quiet enough that I can hear the sharp, sudden increase in my own volume. I clamp down hard, tell myself to lower my voice, but my voice has become its own independent entity in my throat, and it wants to be loud.

"Sebastian—"

"I just want to try something else," I say, too loudly. The stragglers have begun to mill. I can't stop myself. "You can't ask me to do this. You can't tell me to write about this."

"Well, look, the project—"

"And you make it for a *grade*?" I'm heating up, but it's at a remove, as though it's happening to someone else and is, therefore, only mildly interesting. "For a *grade*? What kind of a sadist are you?"

She exhales slowly and nods. "I understand your reaction. I really do. This is supposed to help you learn to think critically. Logically. This doesn't have to be emotionally difficult for you, Sebastian. I'm sure there's another area you could explore, but…if you insist that there's only one thing for you to write on, we can discuss ways to handle the topic of your sister delicately—"

"Don't—"

*Don't talk about my sister!*

**And then there's static everywhere.**

I know I said *Don't talk about my sister*.

No. That's not true. I didn't say it.

I yelled it.

My hand throbs with leftover pain. I hit something.

Some*thing*. Not some*one*. The flat of my palm, smacking against Ms. Benitez's desk. Now I remember. Her stapler jumped.

So did she.

*Don't talk about my sister.*

I blacked out. Went into a fugue state. Sank deep into the static, where sound and light and memory could not find me.

As the static clears, as the world filters in, as the ache in my hand diminishes, I realize I'm in the assistant-principal's office, and he's hanging up the phone, saying, "...of course, thanks," and he looks up at me with eyes like black olives sunk into raw dough. Roland Sperling, the corpulent mass of assistant principal known throughout the student body as the Spermling, regards me like an old hand grenade that has not been deactivated.

"Sebastian, how are you feeling?"

His voice buzzes. Static still clusters at my ears. *Zzze-bazztian, how arezzz you feelingzzz?*

"I'm fine." It takes a moment for my jaw to work properly. It, too, is sore, and I remember like a frame of film: Me, screaming until my voice cracked and then shattered like a wineglass hurled against concrete.

"Are you zzzure about that?" he buzzes.

I claw at my ear to knock away the filter, as though it's a physical thing. The motion accomplishes something, though—the static in my ear goes away, and I can hear normally again.

I screamed at a teacher. I assaulted her desk. These are not things that get wiped away, things ignored and forgotten. I am in serious trouble.

"I'd like to apologize to Ms. Benitez for losing my temper, if I may," I say as calmly as possible. Which, truthfully, is extremely calmly. With the adrenaline out of my system, I've entered a nearly Zen state of relaxation. I am fully aware of my situation, but I can approach it and appreciate it clinically. "My actions were inexcusable," I continue, "but I'd at least like to say I'm sorry to her and offer an explanation. Not an excuse or a justification—just an explanation."

Mr. Sperling steeples his fingers before him. He's been

listening to me with the same regard a big-game hunter gives to a full-tusked elephant.

"I'm sure she'd be receptive to that," he says after a moment's thought, "but first we're going to have you speak to Ms. de la Rosa. I think that would be a good idea. Don't you?"

I think it's actually a terrible idea, but I nod and say, "Of course."

I'm not given a hall pass and sent on my way—Mr. Kaltenbach, one of the gym teachers, escorts me. He just happens to be in the office. It's possible this is a coincidence. It's also possible he was on the receiving end of Mr. Sperling's *of course, thanks*.

We do not speak. We go down the hall, up the stairs, and down another hall, and he wordlessly gestures me into the guidance office before vanishing to wherever it is gym teachers go when not coaxing sweat, regret, and shame from their students.

Ms. de la Rosa, the school's new guidance coun-
selor, is young and right out of college. She has hung
around her office a series of ironic posters, spoofing popular magazine covers with confidence-building headline
remixes. Such as a *Cosmopolitan* cover that blares WHY
YOU'RE PERFECT JUST THE WAY YOU ARE and a *Maxim* that
shouts IN THIS ISSUE: HOW TO RESPECT WOMEN! In short, she
tries too hard.

Last year, soon after she joined the administration, she
summoned me to her office for no obvious reason, though
the nonobvious reason screamed like her unsubtle magazine covers.

After a few minutes of meaningless small talk, I asked
her, "Why did you have me come down here?"

To her credit, she was ready for the question and air-
ily responded, "I'm just trying to get to know the student
body, since I'm new." Almost making it sound as though
I'd won some sort of student lottery, my number drawn
from a hat or selected by computer.

But we both knew what she was doing. Familiarizing herself with the troublemakers, the troubled ones, the troubles, period. Forewarned, forearmed. The best defense and all that.

*Give me the kid back from rehab at noon, the girl who had the baby at Homecoming right after lunch...and to cap off the day, let me get some face time with the guy who killed his baby sister and blocked the whole thing out. That sounds like a full day, right? I'M PERFECT JUST THE WAY I AM!*

Now she smiles at me with a calm learned in years of higher education and practice sessions. No worry lines wrinkle her forehead. Her eyebrows are smooth like an undisturbed pond. Ms. de la Rosa exudes a preternatural sense of self-possession, a force field of Zen. It truly, genuinely disturbs me. No one should ever be this relaxed. It's inhuman.

"How are you feeling, Sebastian? Right at this moment?"

"I'm fine." I give her as little as possible. "I would really like to apologize to Ms. Benitez for my behavior."

"Of course." The smile widens and deepens at the same time. "I think that's a great idea, and you'll get to do that. Keep that one in your back pocket for now, okay? We'll get to it. But right now, I want to know how you're feeling."

"I'm fine," I say again, employing every reserve of willpower I have to keep from adding, "Like I already said."

"Good. Good. No problems with your hearing? Your vision?"

"No. Everything's fine." *Fine* again. It's not *nice*, but its linguistic nutritional value isn't much better. "I feel fine."

"Do you remember yelling at Ms. Benitez? Hitting her desk?"

"I remember enough."

She nods at that. "Enough. Does this happen to you a lot?"

I think of vomiting at Mom's bringing up Lola. Of the rage that picked me up when Mark said "Jihadi Jane." The time that vanished when I read the YouTube comments. And other times in my past. Times when I go away, but I'm still here.

I dodge. "I think it would be appropriate to apologize to her. Don't you?"

"Not yet. Look, we've gotten in touch with your mother, and she's on her way. But I thought maybe we could talk a little bit before she gets here."

Translation: *I drew the short stick, and I get to keep you occupied until your mother gets here with the net and tranq gun.*

A thought occurs to me: Is Ms. Benitez now afraid of me? Is she going to sue me or press charges or something like that?

"I didn't mean to scare anyone. And I didn't want to hurt anyone. I'm a very peaceful guy."

She smiles even more broadly. "I know you are. I know. Do you think maybe we should explore getting you into an English class that might be a little more appropriate for you?"

216

"It's not the class." I try not to bristle, but it's difficult. "I can handle the class. It's just this assignment."

Ms. de la Rosa tilts her head sympathetically. "Sebastian, I can't tell you what to do. I can only show you the road. I can't walk it for you."

Psychobabble. I pretend it's deep and meaningful, something for me to chew over and not just spit out.

"Have you ever…Did you ever discuss hypnosis with your therapist? I'm just wondering. It's not standard, but it's not *not* standard, and I'm just thinking—"

"We discussed it." It comes out a whisper. I know what she'll say next.

"I'm just thinking maybe if you could remember…that might be healing. That might help you get past it."

My throat slams shut midswallow. I stare at my hands, folded in my lap.

"It's Friday," she says. "I'm going to say you should get a jump start on the weekend. Take the rest of the day off."

She makes it sound like a bonus vacation, a stealth holiday that crept out of nowhere and suctioned itself onto my calendar like a facehugger from the original *Alien*, the best one, in my opinion. Seven normal people trapped on a spaceship with a life-form evolved to be the perfect murder machine. So much more terrifying than the jacked-up special effects showcases the later movies turned into.

There's a chirp from her computer. When I look up, she's beaming at me. "Looks like your mom's here."

**I say as little as possible on the way home.**

"I just lost my temper a little bit," I tell her. I don't know what she knows, what Mr. Sperling told her. "It'll be okay. I'm a good student. I have great grades. I've never been in trouble before. They won't throw the book at me."

Mom purses her lips and focuses on driving, saying nothing.

**Mom drops me off at home.** "If I didn't have a meeting, trust me, we'd be having a *very* long talk right now. Don't think you're off the hook. I'll have to stay late to make up for leaving in the middle of the day, but we're having a serious discussion when I get home."

"Hitting a desk isn't the end of the world," I tell her.

"The important thing is *that* you hit, not *what* you hit. As soon as I get home, seriously. The minute I'm through the door." And then she's gone, and I'm alone in the house, and I start laughing. It comes from deep in my gut, welling up like a water spout in the middle of a turbulent ocean, and it takes a terrific effort of will to tamp it down, to turn it into guttural chuckles in lieu of full-blown guffaws.

I can't believe I fell for it.

I can't believe I fooled myself without even trying. That I tricked myself into thinking that I could be happy, that I could be normal, that I could ignore the voice and it would go away, dissipate like smoke in open air. That the voice had gone away, that it ever could go away.

And I realize the voice is screaming at me. No longer whispering. More than that, I realize it's *been* screaming for a while now. I just wasn't paying attention.

But now I am.

Now I am.

*Is it time?*

And the voice says, *Yes. Now.*

It makes perfect sense, suicide does. An end to pain, to misunderstanding. An end to my existence as a walking, talking, living, breathing reminder to my mother of what was taken from her.

Why has it taken me so long? Why have I let my pathetic excuse for a life drag on this long?

I know why. Deep down, I know. I wasn't ready. Not before. Not like I am now. I've been preparing.

I haven't been steeling myself for suicide. The suicide is actually the easy part. It's the other thing.

The other thing. That's what I've been preparing for.

And my phone rings.

**The number is from Florida, according to caller ID.**
There's only one person I know who lives in Florida, and I'm not sure I want to talk to him. I hold the phone in my hand and let it vibrate once, twice, three times. Before it shunts the call to voicemail, I thumb-swipe to answer.

And I pretend.

I'm so good at pretending.

After brief *hello*s, Dr. Kennedy says, "I'm going to be in town this weekend. Do you think you have time to let an old man buy you a Coke?"

This is what he always says when he's coming to town. Dr. Kennedy was my therapist for most of my life—I literally cannot remember a time when I didn't speak to him regularly. About a year ago, he retired and moved to Florida—"Because this is what old people do," he said, somewhat gravely. By then, I was officially done with my therapy, but I still saw him once a month or so. "Just to keep up," he would say.

He moved, but he still comes back to Brookdale two or three times a year, usually in the spring or summer, and each time, he calls me and offers to buy me a Coke. Each time, I tell myself I won't go, that there's no need to. And then that, okay, I'll go, but I won't talk about anything that matters. And each time, he manages to wrangle me into talking about important things, about things that matter, about things that are buried deep—like in a memory hole—and leaves me thinking it was somehow my idea.

He came to Brookdale over the summer, and I genuinely couldn't meet him for that famed Coke; I was too busy with the YouTube channel, and that seems so ridiculous now.

A month ago. And now he's back already.

"This is quite a coincidence," I say casually.

"Not a coincidence at all. I spoke to some people at your school today."

Dr. Kennedy is not a bullshitter or one to conceal. He's bluntly honest, sort of the polar opposite of every psychiatrist on TV and in movies. Popular culture woefully underprepares us for actual therapy. He has never once asked me, "How does that make you feel?" or "What do you think that means?" He's more likely to *tell* me what I feel or what something means.

"You don't have to come up here because of that," I tell him.

"At my age, there aren't many things I *do* have to do. This is something I *want* to do."

"Come on…"

"I didn't get to see you last time I was in town. I keep up with very, very few of my former patients, Sebastian. Did you ever stop to think that I regretted missing you last time, and I'm happy for this opportunity?"

The truth is: No. No, I never stopped to think any of that. Dr. Kennedy has a way of saying something nice that makes me feel guilty, anyway.

"I want us to revisit the question of hypnotherapy."

So. He's definitely spoken to Ms. de la Rosa.

"We've been through it before, Dr. Kennedy."

And we have. So many times. *If you could remember, it might help you get past it.*

And I countered: *Isn't it just as likely that not being able to remember is my way of getting past it?*

*That would be true. If. If you were truly past it. And I don't believe you are.*

"You've refused in the past for very good reasons," he says, "reasons I understand and respect. But I'd like to discuss it again. Can you do me a favor and be prepared to talk about this again, with an open mind?"

And of course I can. Because for Dr. Kennedy I can and would do anything. I promise him to be prepared, to discuss the issue with an open mind, and I hang up and I know it doesn't matter what I've promised because I will not live to have the conversation in the first place.

I'm so *good* at pretending.

I'm a liar.

I've lied to everyone.

To every person in my life, to everyone I know.

I've never told the truth. I've lied to them all.

To my mom. To Evan. To Dr. Kennedy. To Aneesa.

Everyone keeps saying that if I could remember, it would help. That's what they've said all along.

And the thing is this: I remember doing it.
I remember every single bit of it.

# History

I'm told it was a Tuesday.                    It was. This is true.


I'm told it was June and                      Sticky hot and oppressive.
it was hot and there'd                            Unrelenting. Heat like a
been no rain for weeks,                        heavy breath in your face.
no respite from the heat                         Not a whisper of breeze.
that pressed down on
Brookdale.

                    *(bored bored bored)*

I'm told Mom was in the        *Mommy says don't go*      He was cleaning the gun on
backyard, hanging laundry     *outside too hot but Mommy*    the workbench just inside
on the line, that my father    *is outside not fair I want to*   the door that led from the
was in the garage.                    *be outside.*          garage into the house. And
                                                            the doorbell rang and he
                          *(bored bored bored)*             left the gun sitting out as
                                                            he went to answer it.
                         *Daddy says go away I'm*
                          *busy not for little boys*
                               *adult stuff.*


                          *(bored bored bored)*

                        *Doorbell and I go see Daddy*
                           *again but Daddy is not*
                           *there but grown-up toy!*
                             *Grown-up toy!*


229

*Grown-up toy! I have a
grown-up toy!*

*It's heavy and smells funny
like change in Mommy's
pockabook.*

I'm told I leveled my
father's .357 Magnum
at her as she sat in the
little bouncy chair with
the stuffed birds hanging
overhead.

*Go play with grown-up toy.
Go to my room. I hear Lola
in her room. She makes
a song-noise. "So cute"
Mommy says and I say it
too when I hear it.*

She liked to sing along
with the bouncy chair's
recorded music, cooing
off-beat. Over her head,
stuffed birds rotated
slowly on their axes,
captivating her.

*So cute!*

I'm told she would only nap
in the bouncy chair, that
she loved the stuffed birds
and the birdsong that the
chair played for her.

*Go into Lola's room. She's
in bouncy bouncy chair, go
bouncy bouncy. Singsongy
noises.*

She would stare at the
birds and babble her
version of the birdsong for
endless precious minutes.

*Lola sees me. Eyes
wide. Smiles and says
"hah-dah!"*

But then she saw me.

*"Hah-dah! Hah-dah!"*

She couldn't speak, but she could *exclaim*. She could *erupt* with syllables without warning, sometimes blurting out a single sound, then falling silent, other times repeating them in a staccato verbal tattoo over and over.

*Swings her arms and giggles. Bouncy chair jiggles. I laugh too. So cute. So funny.*

*She sees me she smiles her big open toothless smile she smiles with her whole face with every part of her.*

That day, she said, "Hah-dah!"

*Lola is my sister love my sister she's so cute and she loves her big brother Mommy says she loves her big brother.*

God, I remember it.

*Loves when I play with her when I clap for her.*

*She swings her arms again, "Hah-dah! Hah-dah!" Claps her hands.*

I remember it so well. "Hah-dah!"

231

*I swing my arms, clap for her.*

I'm told it was point-blank range and that I shot her one time.

*There's a BIGSOUND and I fall back.*

It was one shot. I don't remember pulling the trigger. Or aiming. I think it was genuinely an accident.

Which, really, is all it takes.

*BIGSOUND. So big! My ears hurt. Ears hurt so much!*

She was four months old. I'm told.

*My ears hurt! Everything hurts! Why am I hurt? I'm shaking. My head hurts, my legs hurt, my arms hurt. I peed in my pants and Mommy will be mad.*

I'm told Mom got there first, the back door being close to the nursery. My father arrived a few seconds later and I was on the floor, blacked out from the kick of the pistol, which knocked me across the room.

*Mommy here now. Mommy! Mommy! I hurt! I hurt! Up, Mommy! Up! Up!*

I didn't black out. Not for an instant. The kick of the Magnum knocked me off my feet, threw me back against the wall. It's a miracle the recoil didn't break my shoulder.

*Mommy not looking at me. Mommy crying and then Daddy screaming and Mommy crying Daddy mad.*

I'm told Mom screamed and screamed, clawing at her own face at the sight before her.

*What happened? What happened?*

*Pee in my pants.*

*Where's Lola? Why is there red?*

Local legend has it that my father, fearing she would gouge her own eyes out or tear her face to ribbons, deliberately punched her out cold.

*Mommy gone. Want Mommy! Everything hurts! Everything hurts all over! WANT MOMMY!*

My father did not punch my mother. He shoved her out of the room. I watched. He shoved her out of the room and cast about, as though looking for something, anything, that was not the tableau before him. Arms outstretched, reaching, grasping, his hands desperate for purchase, to grab hold of reality and warp it, bend it to his will, coming up only with air.

He dropped to his knees near me, keening.

I have no reason not to believe any of the things I've been told.

*Why is there so much red? What happened? What happened?*

Except that so many of them are not true. But the ones that matter *are*.

I could only lay there, dumb and howling in pain and confusion.

I'm told so many things.

*Where's Lola?*

Wondering.

233

I was a child. It was an accident. It wasn't my fault.

*Why is there so much red?*

Not understanding. But I understand now.

I'm told.

*Where's Lola????*

But I've never told.

I was four years old.

*WHY IS THERE SO MUCH RED?*

*WHY IS THERE SO MUCH RED?*

# The Present

**I remember. I've always remembered. There hasn't** been a moment of my life when I haven't remembered.

And it hasn't helped at all.

Which means nothing will ever help.

Which means I'll never get over it. Never never never.

Which means there's only one thing to do.

I've known it all along.

One thing and it's an easy thing, so easy, and I'm so angry at myself for waiting so long. I should have done it years ago. I never should have met Aneesa. I never should have met Evan. I should have been dead so long ago.

Me: Can I come over?

Evan: Now?

Me: Yeah

Evan: 2night's the thing

Me: I know. I just left something at your house
  is all

Me: Five minutes, in and out

Me: No one will know

Evan: OK

**It takes forever to get to Evan's house on my bike.** By the time I get there, on the other side of town, the sun is just starting to dip in the sky, but the heat and the humidity have clung to the dregs of the day and to my back, my forehead, my armpits. I'm exhausted and spent and wet from head to toe, and the only thing that keeps me going is knowing that it's almost over. Almost. So close.

There are half a dozen expensive cars parked in the Danforths' roundabout driveway, and more to come. Evan answers the door in a tuxedo. I try to remember how I should respond to this. Snarky? Faux impressed? I discover that I can't summon the proper reaction, and I fear I'm lost already, but Evan takes one look at me and says, "Jesus, don't let my mom see you, okay?"

On the first Friday evening of the school year, the Danforths throw an expensive, black-tie-only fund-raiser for whichever subject areas or extracurricular activities their offspring have chosen to indulge in that year. It's their way, I'm sure, of compensating their own egos for their children's refusal to attend private schools. When Richard Jr. went to South Brook, the football team was the best funded in the state. Evan is pretty much single-handedly guaranteeing that the drama program and the jazz band will be flush for his four years at South Brook.

The price for this largesse? The Danforth children must attend the soiree, attired appropriately. Hence, Evan's tux. And further hence, the rich people within, with more to arrive soon, explaining Evan's insistence that his mother not see me in my disheveled state.

"Up and down, in and out," I promise. "It's just a DVD I left in—"

"Just go," he stage-whispers, gesturing me in, furtively checking all around to be certain no one notices his poor, underdressed, sweating, stinking buddy.

I scramble up the stairs. I really did leave a DVD here at the beginning of the summer, but I don't care about it.

I only care about Mr. Danforth's office.

About the rifle case.

Everyone is downstairs, drinking unicorn champagne and eating solid gold caviar. Whatever it is rich people do. Me? I'm walking into Mr. Danforth's office like it's my own.

The cabinet is locked, but I know he keeps the key in his desk drawer. Why wouldn't he? His sons are grown and responsible. The lock is just a formality at this point.

I unlock the case. Skip over the rifles. Too big. Unnecessary.

Down at the bottom of the case are the handguns. The big Magnum and the small Colt, the *girly gun*.

I could do all the damage I need to with the Colt, but I take the Magnum. This began with a Magnum and it will end with a Magnum.

I tuck it into my waistband and blouse my shirt over the grip. Even unloaded, it's heavy.

There's a box of ammo, too. I tip a handful of bullets into my palm, then slip them into my pocket.

I drift out of the office and peer over the second-floor balustrade into the vestibule below. It's empty. I have a straight line of escape from here to the front door.

I check the gun again to make sure it won't drop through my waistband and down my pants. Then I head down the stairs, quick and quiet.

My feet have barely touched the vestibule below when another set of footfalls echoes softly from off to the left. I spin just in time to spot a server in a purple bow tie and black suit nearly on top of me, one arm raised to bear a silver platter.

He lowers the platter into my range of vision. "Canapé?" he asks. After a moment in which he takes in my sweaty, disheveled, black-tie-oh-so-optional clothing, he grudgingly adds, "Sir?"

The thought of food causes my stomach to crumple in on itself like a fist. "No, thanks."

He nods and proceeds into the great room. For reasons I don't understand, I pause, wasting a crucial getaway moment to listen for a cry of alarm.

Nothing.

I'm beneath notice.

As it should be.

I dart out the front door and then I'm gone as if I've never been here.

And soon, it will be as though I never were.

**I am going to join Lola in the memory hole.**

It is my proper place. It is where I deserve to be consigned.

Perhaps there's some sort of memory hole equilibrium, and when I go in, Lola will come out. Maybe then Mom will look at pictures and dig out the baby shoes and allow herself to remember. Once she forgets me, maybe then she can remember.

And that, more than anything, will count as me doing something *productive*.

**I almost don't make it. The day has gotten cooler as** night falls, but the air is still and sticky, making it feel hotter.

I coast down one last rise-fall in the road, then drift onto the shoulder, then onto the grass. Almost on inertia, almost like the tide, almost as though the world itself has turned in this specific way at this specific time to make it happen, I glide to the brush and scrub and trees near the trailer.

Hopping off my bike, I let it clatter to the ground. Then I lean against the poplar for a moment, catching my breath. The world spins some more, as the world is wont to do. I close my eyes against its motion, fumble for the Magnum.

It's easy to load. I have more bullets than I need. I load them all anyway.

I take a deep breath, tree bark against my naked neck, tugging at my hair. The abrasion is good. It reminds me I'm alive, that I haven't done it yet, that it still needs to be done.

If only it were raining. It would be the perfect night.

It'll have to do.

My phone has been buzzing and cheeping. Texts and voicemails from Mom, finally home, wanting to know where I am, their character increasingly terrified.

I turn off the phone.

I feel light. Effortless. Gravity has no hold on me.

I'm going to do it. I'm really going to do it.

The last thing I'll do.

I'll do what I need to do.

And then I'll put the barrel in my mouth and angle it up so that the bullet is sure to go through my brain and I'll pull the trigger and at last it will all be over.

There's nothing to stop me.

I'm amazed. There's absolutely nothing to stop me.

I open my eyes. Take up my usual position. I watch the trailer for a moment, just as though this were any other night.

I inhale a deep, long, clean breath. I am pure and holy. The gun weighs nothing in my hand.

I approach the front door.

I knock.

Moments pass.

The door opens.

"Sebastian?"

I say, "Hi, Dad."

**He invites me in.**

Of course he does. I'm his son. Why wouldn't he invite me in?

He doesn't know about the Magnum, now tucked into the waistband of my pants, cool and smooth against the small of my back.

"I can't believe you're here," he says. "Wasn't even sure you remembered where I lived. Been so long."

He stumbles through the trailer. It's not a double-wide, just a plain old trailer, and he seems gigantic within its cluttered confines, a stooping, looming troll from a children's fairy tale, lurching around its own cave.

Sweeping empty chip bags and a dog-eared paperback from a chair, he offers me a seat.

"I'm gonna stand for now."

He nods slowly, resigned, as though accepting a diagnosis. Then he settles himself onto a blue-and-gold love seat that has been weathered by years of the same body in the same spot, contorted into the same angles.

"Can I get you something?" he asks. "I think I have some Coke in the fridge...."

He has sad eyes, my father. I never noticed them before. Or maybe he only allows them to be sad here, in his den, in his pauper's castle, where the air is tangible with sweat and bad dreams and cheap beer and stale chips. Maybe in this place, his armor is at its weakest. Maybe.

"If I'd known you were comin'," he says, filling the air now, clearly discomfited by my silence, "I'da cleaned up a little. Look, it's, uh"—he checks his phone—"not even eight yet. Why don't I take you to dinner or dessert or—"

I can't take it anymore. I thought maybe there would be one last conversation, but I can't take it. I reach behind me, draw the Magnum. It comes loose without friction, and I level it at him.

At this distance, it's nearly impossible to miss him, even with the slight, surprising shake in my hand. I steady the gun with my off hand. My father's face is split by the sight at the end of the barrel.

"Oh, Sebastian," he says.

When I thought of this moment—and I've thought of it often, over the years, obsessing over it, *designing* it in my imagination over and over, tweaking and revising—I imagined him lunging at me, going for the gun. Not that it matters. In such a confined space, when I pull the trigger, he'll take a slug. If the first one doesn't kill him, it will slow him down enough for me to finish him off with the second.

247

And then a third, for myself.

At a distance, it'll be no more than three pops. As remote as the trailer is, no one will suspect anything. Three pops, far off. Two in rapid succession, then a pause, then the third.

I wonder how long it'll take them to find the bodies?

"Oh, Sebastian," he says again. "Son, what are you doing?"

He seems unafraid. He hasn't twitched since I pulled out the gun. He shows no signs of ducking or dodging or leaping for me. If anything, he's settled back into the worn love seat even farther, hands placed on his knees. He shakes his head.

"Talk to me, Sebastian. If you're planning on doing it, talk to me first."

"Why? What makes you think you deserve conversation?" My throat clogs as I speak. I clear it vehemently, disgusted with my body for betraying its human frailty.

"Not saying I do. It's just... don't you think we should at least say good-bye?"

I should say, *I'll say that with a bullet*, and then pull the trigger. Arnold in *Commando*. Sly Stallone in *Cobra*. Eighties tough-guy action movies, unapologetically laden with testosterone and helpless women and groan-inducing comebacks.

And I remember, suddenly, with no warning, the day Dad left. I was six. I clung to him, to his leg. A tear splashed onto the dirty brown leather of his boot. I said, *I don't want you to go.* And he said, *I don't want to go either.*

And I couldn't understand it. If he didn't want to go, then why was he going? Couldn't he just not go, then?

But I didn't say anything. Because it seemed so simple. It was *too* simple. And for years I wondered if I'd been wrong, if I should have said something. If I'd spoken up, if I'd said, "Then don't go," then maybe he would have said, "You're right! That's it!" and stayed. And maybe then we all three could have gotten better together, and he wouldn't have become my personal boogeyman, and the curdled love I felt for him wouldn't have blackened into hate.

"You left. You left us."

"That's not what I did."

"Don't lie to me!" I scream. "You went away! She died and I killed her and you left because of me!"

He shakes his head fiercely. "No. I left because of *me*."

I don't even know what that means. It's adult crap, something adults say to throw us off. I'm tired of it. I'm tired of him. Tired of me. I want it over. I can end it. It's my choice; I'm in control. It's always been my choice, and I've always been in control.

But instead I hear myself say, "Why did you even have that gun?" There's a note of pleading in my voice, and I can't shake it out. "Why was the stupid thing in the house in the first place?"

The gun wavers, even stabilized by both hands. I don't want it to waver; I will it to remain still. Even shaking, the gun sight never leaves my father's face.

"I had it because I had it," he says, his voice heavy and drowning. He's slumped down even farther; there's no way he could get up and come at me without taking two bullets.

"Because you *had* it? What kind of crap excuse is that?"

"Because that's what we do here," he insists, a note of admonition in his voice. I have a gun trained on him and he's admonishing me. "We have guns. We take care of them, and they take care of us, like a good dog, but this dog turned, Sebastian, this dog went rabid and snapped and—"

"The gun didn't turn. The gun didn't do it. *I* did it." The Magnum is getting heavy; it was never designed to be held at full extension like this for so long. I flex my muscles to keep them limber. "I did it. Like what I'm doing now. Don't blame the gun. Blame me. Blame you."

"You don't blame no one for an accident, Sebastian. That's why they're accidents."

"Bull. You left the gun out. I used it. It's *our* fault."

He shakes his head slowly, gnaws at his lower lip. "That what you think? That what you've *been* thinking? All this time? You think it's right to blame a four-year-old for something he can't even understand?"

"You told me to go away. Not to touch the gun. I didn't listen. My fault."

"You're right," he says, now not even looking at me, not even looking at the gun, just staring down at his hands, twisting and turning over themselves in his lap. "But not about it being your fault. But, yeah, it's someone's fault. Damn thing never should have been there. I never should have had it. I wanted to protect us. From what? I don't even know. It's Brookdale, for God's sake. What was I protecting us from? Fucking raccoons?"

When he looks up at me, not blinking or flinching at the sight of the gun still leveled at him, his eyes are red and wet.

"You don't get to cry. Not for her." I struggle for a moment, the gun too heavy. Then I recover and my aim is true. "You don't have the right."

"Maybe not. Can't help it, though. In the morning, your mother would bring her into the bedroom. To nurse her. For breakfast, you know?"

"I don't care."

"And she'd lay her down in the bed next to me," he goes on, as though the person with the *gun* hadn't said a word, "and I'd look over at her and she'd look over at me, and she would stare for a second and then she'd break into this huge smile. Like she was thinkin', *Oh, this guy! I remember this guy!* And I swear, it was the best part of my day. Everything else, no matter what happened that day, it

252

was downhill. Had to be. Because I had the best thing in the world first thing in the morning. Such a lucky bastard. I got the best thing in the world when I opened my eyes every morning."

Against my will, I think of her, of Lola. I shove the memory away, but it comes back, and maybe that's the way it should be. I should be thinking of her when I do it. My vision blurs with tears, but it doesn't matter—the shimmery shape of my father is still at the end of the gun sight.

"Best thing in the world. And someone rings the doorbell and I don't even think, Sebastian. I don't even *think*!"

I blink, blink, blink. Tears drop. My father's hands are clenched into fists and he beats one of them on the arm of the love seat. *Thum. Thum.*

"I just go answer the goddamn door! Like I'm a robot! Ding-dong! Coming, master! Fuck! Leave the gun right there. I was cleaning it and I was done and I'd loaded it because, hey, it was for protection, right? It was for protection, and what good is it if you have to load it in the middle of the night? And I just left it there and went to the door, and it was some goddamn Jehovah's Witness, and by the time I got rid of him…"

My father is in my sights, but all I see is Lola. He is warped by tears into Lola.

"I'm headed back to the gun, thinking, *Oh, crap, I can't believe I did that.* Thinking, *That was close,* and I hear … Oh, shit." He shakes his head viciously. "No," he says. And again. "No." And over and over, and my lips move with his, silently repeating his *No*.

And then my father, a big man with hard, square working hands, a man who wears armor even when he's naked, breaks down. He bawls like a child who's been hurt for the first time, no reserve, no restraint. No shame. Tears explode from him; great sobs wrack his body; his chest heaves uncontrollably.

"Jesus. Jesus. Jesus. Oh, fucking Jesus." There's no Jesus here. Jesus doesn't want to be here in this dingy shit-trailer, in this hovel of desperate, slovenly contrition. Jesus has abandoned us; God, too. There's no one to watch. No one to care. No one to offer absolution.

Except.

"My kid was dead," he blubbers. "She was dead, and it was my fault and it's everywhere, it's on the news, it's in the papers, it's online, and you know what some liberal blogger asshole says online? Some fucking asshole from up north? He says, *The best solution to a bad toddler with a gun is a good toddler with a gun*. He says, *If only the little one had been armed*." He grabs at his hair, his beard, pulling, clawing. "My kid is fucking dead and it's my fault and I'm grieving and he's making fucking *jokes*, that cocksucker!"

He stands, springing up from the love seat so quickly that I don't even react, arms outstretched, and he screams, "So *do it, then!*"

If only it were raining.

Ten years ago, I raised a gun and I fired.

If it were raining, it would be a perfect night.

*Do it, then!* my father cried, and the voice inside me shouted it at the same time.

And I can't.

I can only do it by accident.

And the gun falls from my numb fingers and I collapse, weeping, into my father's arms.

**The gun lies on the shabby throw rug,** glimmering in the middling light of my father's trailer. I lie crumpled in my father's arms, the two of us wrapped together, now on the love seat, weeping against each other, snorting, snuffling. From somewhere, he's produced a handkerchief, which he hands to me. I accept it and wipe my swollen eyes, blow my nose. I hand it back to him.

"I was going to kill you," I whisper, "and then kill myself."

He tightens his embrace. Kisses the top of my head as though I'm a child. And I am. Of course I am.

"I'm sure," he says. "And you think that would have fixed things?"

Would it have? Billions of people in the world; billions of planets around billions of stars in the universe. Would removing my father and me from the map of reality have changed anything? Two fewer lives in a world that never acknowledged them much in the first place. Would it matter?

"I wouldn't have felt bad anymore. It would have fixed that."

"What about your mother? How do you think *she* would have felt?"

"She got over Lola. She could get over me. It would be easier, without me."

"Sebastian," he says quietly, twisting out of our tangle, holding me at arm's length. Staring into me. "Sebastian, look at me, son. Your mother ain't gotten over Lola. You know that as well as I do. You know she ain't gotten over it, and she never will. Just like I never will. And, yeah, Sebastian, I'm sorry, but you never will neither. It ain't how people are built."

"So we just go on like this? Feeling like shit for the rest of our lives?"

It's the first time I've ever sworn in front of my father. He pretends not to notice.

"We all deal with it in our way. Your mom, she can still function, see? That's good. That's a good thing. Someday, she'll be on the other side of the clouds. On the other side of the storm. She'll be able to look behind her and see the darkness. And she'll always be aware of it, and it'll always be there, hovering, but it'll be *behind* her, see? You'll get there, too."

"But not you."

He says nothing, still staring at me. Then he breaks away, pulls back. Looks up at the ceiling. "You'd pulled that trigger, maybe. But, no. I'll never come through. I don't deserve to."

"I want you to come home." The words surprise me; that I mean them surprises me even more. And I'm weeping again, snotty and teary like a little boy.

He carefully folds the handkerchief to expose a clean panel and hands it back to me, saying nothing as I blow my nose and wipe my eyes again. I can't look at him.

"I can't come home," he says. "There ain't a home for me there no more."

"Mom still has your things. She hasn't thrown them out."

"Home's not about things. I don't expect you to understand. Home is something else. You and your mom, you've made a home. You've repaired a home. You don't need me coming in there."

Need…"Yeah, but what if we *want* you?"

He smiles sadly and nods. "You sure you're speaking for both of you?"

I have no answer for that. I don't know how it happened, how it all fell apart. There were the fights, but people fight. And there was Lola, but sometimes those things drive families closer, not farther apart.

Why couldn't we be one of those families? Why do we have to be us?

"I just want something normal," I tell him. "I just want to feel normal."

"I'm proud of you for not pulling that trigger," he says softly. "That had to be a hard decision to make. And if you'd only come here to kill me, that might have been okay. But you got a whole life to live."

"For Lola."

"No!" His outrage is immediate and wounded; he heaves and I flinch. "No! Not for her! For *you*. Your job is to live for yourself, Sebastian. You only get one life. You get one...one *chance*."

*Shot*. He was going to say *one shot*.

"One chance." He sniffs. "One chance to close the door, to ignore the bell, to put it away. One fucking chance. Don't blow yours. Don't carry the burden. That ain't your job. It ain't for you to carry her."

"Then who does?"

He wipes a tear from his eye. "Leave that to me."

I look at the gun, still on the floor. He looks, too.

"Where did you get that?"

I tell him. Where. How. When.

He sighs and checks his watch. "All right, then. I'll get it back there. Make sure no one ever knows."

"How?"

"Don't matter how. I'll figure it out. Party's still going on. No one's paying attention. I..." He shakes his head. "Just don't worry about it. It's the least I can do. I'll take care of it." He stoops to pick up the gun. For some reason, I expect him to pluck it gingerly, to take the very edge of the grip between his thumb and forefinger, to hold it from its tail like a dead rat.

But instead he grabs it up, points it at the ceiling, flips open the cylinder, and empties each chamber. Checks that it's empty, then double-checks. All done with cool efficiency, bloodless confidence. He puts the ammo in his pocket and jams the empty gun into his waistband. When he turns to look at me again, it's with the look of a gunslinger.

"I can't stop you from killing yourself. If that's what you truly want, no one can stop you. I can't be around twenty-four hours a day, looking after you. But if that's what you want, don't you think you owe it to your mother to talk to her first?"

Mom: Where are you?

Mom: Where are you?

Mom: Where did you go?

Mom: You're not answering. Pick up when I call
you!

Mom: Left you another voicemail. Where are
you?

Mom: Called Evan. He said you were there a
little while ago. Where are you?

Mom: I'm calling the police.

Me: On my way home

**Mom looks older than her usual old. She's frail and** weak, still in her work clothes even though she usually changes as soon as she gets home. I think she wants to be very, very angry, but relief is etched into every line of her face.

"Where have you been?" She comes down hard on *been*, biting into it, bruising the word, punishing it in a way she cannot punish me.

"I went to see Dad."

It hangs in the air between us, hovering like a will-o'-the-wisp before settling.

"I see."

She turns from me and heads into the living room. I follow.

"You can't just disappear like that. Especially after what you pulled in school today. And you have to answer me when I—"

"Mom, I had to talk to him about Lola."

For a moment, she's frozen in the center of the room. Then the moment cracks like thin ice and she regains her poise; she sits on the sofa. "That's still no excuse," she says. I can tell she's rattled, though, and a spring of pity for her bubbles up from deep inside me. This has been a day of too much for her—for me, too, but I can handle it—and she's not ready for even more.

But Dad was right: I need to talk to her. I need her to understand.

"You need to let me know where you are," she says, now wringing her hands and staring at the coffee table. "You can't just run off."

"Mom, I remember."

Her hands pause for an instant, then resume. She does not look up at me. "Well, next time remember to text me back, or at least to—"

"That's not what I mean, Mom. I mean, I remember that day."

She nods. She nods. She nods again. And again. Her head bobs fiercely and still she does not look up. Her hands tighten on each other, squeezing each other dead white.

I don't know how to do this. Mom and I don't talk. Not really. She brings it up, I retreat. I bring it up, she retreats. We're never in sync. We're like a broken strobe light.

"How long?" she asks, a whisper I strain to hear. "When did you remember?"

Oh. Hands jammed in my pockets, I shrug. "Always. I've always remembered. I just never told anyone."

Finally, she looks at me. Her chin trembles, jaw

working in spastic tics. "Oh, Sebastian. God, Sebastian. Why?"

"I don't know." But I do know. Because I was four. Because I understood I'd done something very, very Bad. I knew it made people upset and angry. So it was easier to pretend I didn't remember doing it. The kind of logic only a four-year-old can appreciate, the kind of logic I stumble to explain to her. "And then I was stuck with it. And every day, week, year, whatever, it just seemed easier and easier to pretend."

She opens her mouth to speak, but can't. Flaps her hands instead, gesturing me closer, and I sit next to her and she throws her arms around me and pulls me in close. There is still strength in her too-old limbs; she crushes me to her and whispers, "Oh, Sebastian," over and over.

"I have to talk about it, Mom."

She pulls back and shakes her head viciously. "You were a toddler, for God's sake. It's not your fault. You can't blame yourself. Stop it."

"I need to talk about it. I need to know what it was like. For you. Dad told me. I didn't realize I needed it until he did, but I need to know. I barely knew her."

"Stop it." Shaking her head again. So violently.

"I just want to know, Mom. Please."

"Sebastian, you're my son and I love you and I would do anything for you, but I can't do this. I'm sorry," she says with finality, withdrawing to the other end of the sofa.

"I can't talk about this. I can't relive this. I'm not strong enough."

"You think *forgetting* her makes it better? Pretending? Look at you! You're a hermit, Mom! You never leave the house, except for work and your therapist. You got rid of the pictures and all the mementos, but you can't get rid of her, no matter how much you try."

She stiffens. "Good night." She heads to the hallway.

"Mom!" I'm up off the sofa. "Stop doing this to yourself! To us!" I use my last weapon. "Dad can do it. Dad told me what I wanted to know. I just need—"

She spins to me so suddenly that I take a step back, connect with the coffee table, nearly spill backward onto it. Her eyes, red-rimmed, pin me in the air, and her face twists into an ugly, contorted mask.

"You need? You need? What about what I need? All I've done is think about what you need for ten years. Your father couldn't handle it; he left. He got to go. I had to stay. Stay here, in this house, walking past that door every day and every night, remembering. I didn't get to escape, Sebastian."

"Mom…" I hold up my hands, palms out. "Calm down…."

"Calm down? Calm down? No, Sebastian." She steps closer to me. "This is what you want. You want to talk. You want to know how I feel."

Mom's throat works; I'm close enough to see the tendons clutch and spasm.

"Dad said you used to bring her into the bedroom every morning to—"

"Stop it!" she screams, hands to her temples, as though her head has split open and she has to hold it closed. "Just stop it!"

It's such a sudden change that I should be shocked, but I'm not. I realize what I've done—I've injected a memory too strong for her to ignore, too powerful, too primal. And I should stop here, but I can't.

"I can't! I've spent my whole life not talking about it, and where has that gotten me?"

"It got you this far! You have friends and school and—"

"Friends? Are you crazy? I have one friend, Mom: Evan. Aneesa isn't talking to me because I ruined that, and you know why? Do you know why? Because I'm so messed up that I can't deal with other people like a normal human being!"

"You've had therapy," Mom snaps. "You can have more. You're the one who refused to see someone else after Kennedy retired. I can't wipe your nose for you anymore, Sebastian. You're not a—a child."

*Baby*.

"Jesus Christ, Mom, look at you! You can't even say the word *baby*. This is healthy to you? This is normal? This is okay?"

She snorts and spits out her words, staccato: "No, it's not, but I'm doing the best I can."

"Well, you're doing a shit job of it."

Eyes wide and flashing, she purses her lips into a tight ring of anger. "You don't get to tell me how to be a parent."

I've pushed her too far. I've backed her into a corner from which there's no escape and no respite. And I recognize this. Some part of me that still thinks recognizes this, but I keep battering at her anyway.

"Your way isn't working. We can't keep pretending—"

She throws her hands up in the air. "Jesus, Sebastian. I'm doing the best that I can. What do you *want* from me?"

"The truth!"

"The truth? The truth is that I'm barely holding myself together, okay? The truth is that I alternate between being so sad I could melt away and so angry I could explode. Are you happy now? Does that make it all better? Do you think that's going to *change* something? That's going to undo it?"

I should stop. I shouldn't keep going.

"She's *dead*, Mom. She's your daughter and she's dead. So yeah, you're angry and sad, but come on, you're holding back, you're always holding back, and I do, too, but I don't want to anymore, I just want you to—"

"I hate you!" Her arms locked at her sides, fists clenched, eyes screwed tightly shut, she screams it at the top of her voice. "Are you happy now? Is that what you want to hear? I hate you I hate you I HATE YOU! You killed her! You murdered my little baby girl! I hate you, Sebastian—God, I fucking hate you!"

And she shoves me in the chest, but I'm locked in place, so she just collapses there on the floor. She's a ball of tears and snot and horror and agony and fear and the sort of pain that starts in the gut and spreads out in both directions until it consumes you from head to toe, inside and out.

And there's nothing for me to do but to kneel beside her. "That's okay," I tell her.

I tell her, "That's okay," and then I say the words I've been waiting to say since I was four years old, the words I've said to everyone in my life except for her, the words I can't stop saying until she's around, when a blast door slams down over my tongue and the words are stuck on the other side.

I say, "I'm sorry."

She howls like a wolf cut loose from the pack. The howl is an awful thing, a living thing with its own corrupt and bleak soul, a hopeless thing, lost, its destination burned to the ground, its home blighted.

Sobbing, she claws at her eyes, and I remember that moment from ten years ago, Dad shoving her. Gentler, I take her wrists in my hands and pull her fingers away from her face. Her eyes are swollen and red, painful, rimmed with tears and running makeup.

"Don't," she says.

"Mom, I have to talk about it. I have to, okay? I can't go on like this. I've been—" *thinking of killing myself* is the end of that sentence, but not something I can say to her. Not yet. Not even now.

"I've been so sad," I say instead.

She folds me in her arms. I fold her in mine.

**Later, she's fallen asleep on the sofa. We've been** talking for hours, and it's past three in the morning, and I'm so tired I can't sleep, so I sit up in the easy chair and watch her instead.

"Shouldn't have said it," Mom mumbles, rousing.

"What?"

She blinks her eyes clear. It takes a few seconds for them to focus on me. "What I said. Before. I shouldn't have said it."

"It's okay."

"It's not. I'm your mother. And besides, it wasn't true. It isn't true. None of it."

"I don't believe that."

"Sebastian..."

"Be honest with me, Mom."

She sits up, fruitlessly tries to straighten her wrinkled and disheveled work clothes. Gives up.

"It was true," she admits. "Once. At one time. For a *moment*. And I couldn't say it, couldn't let myself think it, because it was awful."

"I hated myself, too."

She strokes my cheek. "Don't hate yourself, sweet-heart. It gets you nothing. It gets you nowhere."

"I know." Now.

She sighs and rubs her eyes. "After it happened, maybe a year later, I told myself I was going to be one of those moms....One of those moms who bounces back from tragedy, who changes the world. Like the ones who started Mothers Against Drunk Driving. But I learned something. I'm not strong, Sebastian. Those people are the exception. I'm not exceptional. Most of us hide. Most of us just curl up and hide. So I did nothing."

"You kept us together."

"I couldn't even do that. Your father left."

"Yeah, but you still let him see me. Even when I didn't want to. You did your best."

She shrugs. "How do you feel now?"

"Tired."

"Me too."

We laugh together. "Good thing it's Saturday tomor-row."

"It's Saturday right now," I remind her.

She rises, smooths her skirt. "Well, it'll still be Satur-day later, after we get some sleep."

"There's just one more thing."

I can almost hear her throat constrict, can almost hear her thinking, *What the hell else could there be?*

"Why did you get rid of everything?" I ask. "Why did you just delete her from our lives?"

She walks away. Before I can react, she's back, with her purse, rummaging inside.

"All the pictures and stuff are at Gramma's house. There was no way I threw it out. Not a chance. I just couldn't be surrounded by it. And I didn't want you surrounded by it. This is all I have with me."

She produces her phone from the depths of her purse. Flicks it on. Scrolls to a photo. "This is the one I let myself look at. This is the day we brought her home from the hospital."

It's a picture of Lola, tiny and wrinkled, her face a tight little fist, her eyes screwed shut against the world. Somehow, though, she's relaxed. At peace.

Content.

Holding her is four-year-old Sebastian, beaming at the camera as it goes off.

"That's good," I try to say, but my voice is drowned in tears.

"She loved her big brother from the beginning," Mom manages to say, and kisses my forehead.

**People have been telling** me that "time heals all wounds" my entire life. I never really believed them—scabs and scars form, I figured, but I didn't imagine that the wounds themselves ever truly healed. They just lurk beneath the new surface, as raw and as sensitive as the day they were made. They're just not visible any longer. They're just not exposed.

I'm still not ready to believe time heals wounds, but I think maybe something else does.

*We* heal wounds. Not time.

Us.

Evan has never said anything about the gun, so I assume Dad managed to sneak it back in somehow. I have no idea how. I see him every week now, and one time I asked him. He just shrugged and said, "I have my ways."

I said, "So...you're a ninja?"

He did a little karate chop. And he smiled.

He actually smiled. It was small and brief, but it was there.

**A school is a big place; it's easy to avoid each other.** A school bus is big, too—one of you in front, the other in back, the distractions of friends and the driver's terrible choice in radio stations. A school bus can be a stadium, and you can get lost in there, if you're willing. If you try hard enough.

So, a day or two before Halloween, on a Sunday, I bike up to Aneesa's for the first time in a long time. I haven't seen her since I told her to get out of my room. I actually only said, "Get out," never specifying. In that moment, I meant my room, my house, my heart, my life. She honored my request and vacated them all as best she could.

When I knock at the door, Mr. Fahim answers. I wonder what he knows, how much he knows. I wonder at the character of his knowledge; how did Aneesa tell the story? Was I the sick and injured prince or the outraged and out-of-control dragon?

"Ariadne," he says with a slight quirk of his lips. "Aneesa isn't home."

"Oh." I turn back to my bike.

"You're welcome to wait for her, if you like."

I don't like, but I have no choice. If I leave now, I'll never work up the courage to come back again. I need to do this now.

Reluctantly, I trudge inside. Everything has finally been unpacked. Artwork and photographs hang on the walls. The Fahims have completed the metamorphosis of the house no one wanted to buy into a home.

"We haven't seen you around here lately," Mr. Fahim says, gesturing for me to sit in one of the living room chairs. He takes the sofa.

"Well, school…" I let it drift and hang, smoke in the open air.

"Aneesa has been making new friends. I assume you've been busy with old ones."

I let him think that.

"Do you believe in the afterlife?" he asks suddenly.

"I'm not sure." I don't want to offend him. And it's a tough question for me. I'd love to see Lola again, but I also figure I probably don't deserve that.

"Many don't. Because it offends them to imagine all this"—he gestures around us, to the world beyond the room—"is a mere test. But it isn't a test. It's a trial. To determine if we are worthy. So it's nothing we should shrug off, regardless of what follows. How we are now, to one another, dictates our eternity."

I follow him, but I'm not sure how it's relevant, until I realize what the whole point is: He knows. Either Aneesa told him or someone else did. He knows.

"What I mean to say," he goes on, "is this: Life is short, but its brevity does not mean it's meaningless. Work out your differences with Aneesa, whatever they are."

"I'd like that."

Mr. Fahim sighs. "I like you a great deal, Ariadne. And I understand better than most, I think. I'm very happy with Sara. I adore my wife and the life we have. So I don't mean to insult you, when I say that…in an ideal world, I would see Aneesa with a Muslim boy. You understand?"

I shrug a noncommittal *yes*.

"But this is not an ideal world. You two are good together. And I would be happy if someday—in the future, you understand—if that turned into something more."

"I don't think that's in the cards, sir."

"It's still Joe. And I'm sorry to hear that." He takes a deep breath and glances around, as though for spies. "I am her father and I'm not supposed to say such things, but I will." He gazes directly into my eyes. "Her loss."

**Aneesa and her mother arrive home to find Joe and** me fragging aliens in *Halo*. I suck at it, my reflexes dulled from years of Intellivision and Atari 5200 games. Mr. Fahim doesn't care. He claims I'm better than his wife, but not as good as Aneesa, which is "the sweet spot."

Aneesa seems rattled to see me. A silent communication passes between her and her father, then her father and her mother, and then the adults leave us alone together in the living room.

"How are you doing?" she asks.

I've imagined this moment for a while now, speaking both sides of the conversation in my head, configuring and reconfiguring her responses and my responses to her responses, constructing a conversational flowchart designed to land me at the optimal conclusion.

And in an instant, I toss it out. Small talk and caution will get me nowhere.

"You told me the truth," I tell her, "the last time we saw each other."

"Not all of it," she says, interrupting my flow.

"What do you mean?"

She fidgets for a moment. Then: "Look. I was afraid. Moving here. It's not exactly—"

"Not exactly the most diverse place."

"Yeah. And I was worried about fitting in, and I grabbed hold of the first friend I could find. And then we actually became good friends. *Such* good friends. And I felt bad that you wanted more...."

"Don't worry about... Look, just... It's time for me to tell *you* the truth."

From my pocket, I produce five sheets of paper, stapled together. I hand them to her.

Without a word, she scans the top sheet. Says "Oh" very quietly. And then she reads.

I guess I had hoped—or some part of me had, in any event—that it would make her cry. It doesn't. It just makes her quiet for a long time, longer than it takes to read.

Finally, she speaks: "So, not to put pressure on you or anything, but I totally have an idea for a new pizza." The bounce and the lilt of her voice are like a balm, like a good memory too long neglected.

"Since when do you come up with the recipes?" I challenge her.

"Hear me out: deconstructed pizza."

I blink, then grin. I can already see it: thin wafers of

crust with a tomato dipping sauce and cheese wheels on the side. "Derridare I?" I ask her.

Just like I knew she would, she catches my Derrida pun and fires back: "I de Man you do so!"

She returns my grin, and for an instant, none of it ever happened. Which is wrong because our lives are the sum of our mistakes as well as our triumphs, right?

But the grin is good and so is mine, and it feels right, and then she sighs and brandishes the rolled-up papers. "This, by the way?"

"You don't have to say anything."

We wallow in a moment of blissful silence.

And she looks up at me, impassive for a moment before the eyebrows arch in that Aneesa way, and she says, "You're pretty much the best person I've ever known. I wish I were in love with you."

"That's okay."

"Are you really going to turn this in for a grade?"

I nod. "Tomorrow."

# Tomorrow

Sebastian Cody
ACAS Assignment
October 28
Period 1

**Assignment: Write a personal essay about a significant event in your life, and what you would or would not change about it.**

### *BOY, 4, SHOOTS, KILLS INFANT SISTER*

That's what you want to hear about, isn't it? That's what you want to know. You want to know what happened and how it happened, the things that don't make it into the news, the things that never leave my head, the things my mother said, the things my father did.

But you don't get those things. They're not yours.

And besides: That moment was not my most influential. That moment does not define me. I've never even read that article, only the headline.

When I was four years old, I killed my baby sister. It was an accident, but not the sort that you can apologize for and fix. You cannot repair this mistake; it lives on.

So do I.

I thought my sister was consigned to the memory hole, that she'd been erased from the world as a consequence of my actions. But I've come to realize recently that even the things in the memory hole still existed. They still happened. Just because Big Brother tried to make them disappear forever didn't mean they never existed in the first place, no matter how well-executed the erasure. If there's one Winston who defies Big Brother and fails, there will be another who succeeds. Someone has to destroy and re-create the documents. Someone knows. Someone remembers.

Everyone thinks "poor kid." Everyone thinks "Thank God that's not me." But you know what? I'm okay being me. No matter how bad it's been for me, it's been worse for someone else.

This essay is supposed to prepare me to think about myself critically, a way of examining myself in preparation for writing a college application. So I want to say this: Any college that wants to hear about something that happened when I was four years old—any person who wants to hear about it—is crazy. It's impossible to apply autocriticism or self-reflection to something so remote.

And it's also ridiculous to expect teenagers to have a "significant event" in their lives that is even worth writing an essay about. Some will, but most won't. And as a consequence, your end result is essays that inflate the common and the mundane into the spectacular and the unexpected, all to meet the criteria of an assignment whose value is dubious at best. It's encouraging solipsism of the worst sort. Better off asking us to describe some significant world event and how we responded to it. Or some small event that no one cares about, but we do, and then explain why.

Because here's something else that I've learned—rarely do the "significant events" in our lives change us. At least, not in any way we want. The people who suffer tragedy and go on to greatness? They're the stuff of movies and TV shows and books, and—only very rarely—real life. Most of us just go on, the walking wounded, dealing with our lives. This doesn't make us bad—it just means we're not superheroes. It means we're just people, like everyone else.

But I'll bite. I'll play.

In the summer between my freshman and sophomore years, I met someone new in my neighborhood: Aneesa. We quickly became friends. We bonded over a mutual sense of humor and a love of pizza, yes, but I think we bonded more over our differences than our similarities.

I'm not religious, but I'm told that's God's point. If so, I applaud God's thinking.

She was funny and quick-witted, and she cared for me in a way I wasn't used to, a way I couldn't really process. She laughed at my jokes even when they weren't funny. She listened to me and didn't try to fix things. She was open and kind, and when she raised her eyebrows, I thought my heart would stop beating in my chest. Unconditional acceptance. She wasn't afraid to look at the darkness and keep smiling. Unlike everyone else, who either looked and then looked away, ashamed, or gawked.

But more important, she was different. She was like no one I'd ever met before. And, to my shame, I allowed that to consume me. I was so used to being an outcast that I thought only of what made her different, too, thinking that this bonded us, that I couldn't possibly have anything to offer other than commiseration.

And I fell in love with her. Far too hard and far too soon. And I just assumed that the feelings were reciprocated. Not really because of anything she did—though I convinced myself certain things mattered more than they did—but mostly because that's what I needed in the moment.

I treated her like a remedy, not a person.

Someone told me at one point that Aneesa
had put me in the friend-zone. Which everyone
knows is a horrible place to be. If you've ever
seen the old movie *Superman II* (from 1980, and if
you haven't, you should—the Donner Cut is
particularly righteous), you can imagine the friend-
zone as being like the prison where they keep the
villains from Superman's home planet—a flat,
featureless mirror-like surface that spins and wheels
through space for eternity, with no way out. All
you can do from there is look out into the
universe and see what you don't have, what you
can't have, what you'll never have.

She and I built something together,
something not just cool, but also worthwhile.
Productive, even. And fun. And I'm not going to
let it go away just because of the past. I won't let
history topple tomorrow.

So, what is my significant event? I'm
getting there. All of this critical self-reflection
takes time. If it were quick and easy, what would
be the point?

We—*all* of us—keep pigeonholing each
other. *Muslim girl eats pizza* is somehow more
compelling than *girl eats pizza*. Or just *person eats
pizza*. Harry Potter is the boy who lived, and
I'm the boy who killed. Aneesa wears hijab and

everyone thinks they know who and what she is.
Friend-zoned is worse than boyfriend.

And it's all crap. Because I'm also the boy
who invents pizzas, and she's funny and fun and
plays a mean oboe and—despite what some idiots
say—is not out to destroy America.

I realize now that she made it possible for me
not to think about other things, things I'm not
going to talk about in this essay because they're
none of your business. They're no one's
business. And that, truly, is the major
life-changing moment I'm writing about.
My epiphany, if you will.

Some things are private. And they should stay
that way and they get to stay that way. This isn't
preschool; I don't have to share.

I don't have to tell unless I want to. My
"significant events" can be personal and hidden
and they're still real. They still count, even if
I don't perform an autopsy on them in order to
please you or some college admissions board.
They're still mine and they still matter, even if
I'm not willing to take out my Aztec ceremonial
mosaic-handled knife and sacrifice them on the
altar of the almighty God of Grades.

The word *autopsy* is just a letter-swap away
from being *auto-spy*. I'm not going to spy on

myself for you. Big Brother has enough Thought Police. He doesn't need me informing on myself.

That's what I learned: People can wonder and ponder and imagine all they want. But their curiosity does not entitle them to enter my world.

One other thing I learned, and this one may be even more important: The key word in "friend-zone" is *friend*.

# LOWE COUNTY TIMES

## *Boy, 4, Shoots, Kills Infant Sister*

**BROOKDALE, MD.**—Police and EMTs responded to a 911 call on Tuesday night on Fox Tail Drive, where a four-year-old boy shot his infant sister, aged four months, in the head. According to police, the toddler was playing with a gun left unattended by his father. The infant was pronounced dead at the scene.

Prosecutors are declining to discuss the incident as the investigation is ongoing, but it is believed no charges will be brought. The boy's name is being withheld since he is a minor. Consequently, the *Times* will not reveal the names of the parents, as that would expose the child.

———————

# Acknowledgments

I can't get anything done without the people who tolerate me on a daily basis and make it possible to write in the first place.

Thank you to Morgan Baden, Eric Lyga, and Paul Griffin, beta readers *par excellence*.

Thank you, too, to my agent, Kathleen Anderson, for always pushing her hardest, both on the books themselves and for the benefit of my career.

My editors on this book, Alvina Ling and Allison Moore, questioned me where I needed to be questioned and pushed where I needed to be pushed. Thank you so much.

Thanks also to Nikki Garcia, Kheryn Callender, Victoria Stapleton, Jessica Shoffel, Marisa Finkelstein, Jeff Campbell...the whole team at Little, Brown, especially the folks in Marketing, Sales, Publicity, and Production. It takes a *lot* of people to make a book...and the LB people are the best.

# Special Thanks

I'm not a Muslim. So I've relied on research and honest talk for my portrayal of Aneesa and her family.

I am forever indebted to Zohra Ashpari, Kaye M., Ardo Omer, and my dear friend Daniel Nayeri for their time, understanding, and generosity.

This is fiction and I'm not perfect, so I'm sure I've made mistakes. Hopefully, they aren't big ones.

# DISCUSSION GUIDE

1. What were your first impressions when you started reading? Why is the first-person narrator so powerful for this story?

2. Why is the book divided into the sections "History," "Present," and "Tomorrow"? What effect does this narrative structure have on the story while reading? What other unique narrative features did you notice?

3. What is the importance of Sebastian's friendship with Aneesa? How is it different from his friendship with Evan? Why is the timing of his new friendship with Aneesa significant?

4. Sebastian describes his room as "a museum to the old, to the things I love." How does his room contrast with the rest of his house? How does he treat memories differently than his family? Why does Sebastian say his sister is in the memory hole, and does it affect how he treats his own things?

5. Why does Sebastian wait so long to tell Aneesa about his sister? Do you think it was a good idea?

6. This book is described as "ripped from the headlines." Why is this story so important for people to read? What impact did it have on you emotionally?

7. Sebastian admits that he never believed the adage "Time heals all wounds," but has found a different kind of solution. Why is that phrase so commonly used as advice? Do you ag███ ██ Sebastian?

8. ██ ████ ████████ ████spaper article at the end? Does ████████ ███ reader? Why or why not?

# Resources for Help

**Dark thoughts? Thinking of suicide?**
National Suicide Prevention Lifeline
1-800-273-8255
suicidepreventionlifeline.org
Specifically for Youth:
suicidepreventionlifeline.org/help-yourself/youth/

Live Chat @ ImAlive
imalive.org

American Foundation for Suicide Prevention
afsp.org

**Ending Gun Violence**
The Brady Campaign to Prevent Gun Violence
bradycampaign.com

Be SMART
besmartforkids.org

Moms Demand Action for Gun Sense in America
momsdemandaction.org

**Report a Hate Crime**
First, contact local law enforcement.
Then: Southern Poverty Law C
splcenter.org/reporthate